My

Nemesis

THE MIND'S EYE

Cover Design by Aija M. Butler

Cover Photos ©Dreamstime

mynemesisbkseries@gmail.com

http://mynemesisthebkseries.blogspot.com

www.twitter.com/NemesisBkSeries

ambpublishing@gmail.com

http://ambpublishingpr.blogspot.com

Book Dedication

This Book is Dedicated to My Beloved Brother, Arnold Blair Muckleroy, AKA Boov 5000
An Author of Music, Poetry and Wisdom
July 2, 1986-December 21, 2010
"In Life, you should live and pursue goals and dreams that are your own make you happy, say... I did that, I Do Me..."

Armie

~THE MIND'S EYE~

WEATHER THE STORM

~1~

Conscious

Joy gasped as the inhalation of the open air hit her seemingly virgin lungs. Abruptly she awoke buried deep into an abyss of darkness. She feared she was abducted. Joy was unable to open her eyes. She began to panic tussling around moving her fingers in search of clues to her surroundings. Joy's arms and legs burned as she tried to free herself. Her eyes moved rapidly under her lids. She was afraid; but fought to calm herself as she called her attention to the footsteps approaching.

Joy swallowed hard and braced herself as best she could as the quickening steps moved closer to her.

"Good morning Mrs. Anderson, we are elated that you are awake."

"Where am I?" Joy was groggy and in desperate need of water. Her body ached she moaned and groaned trying to adjust herself to a comfortable position.

"Mrs. Anderson, are you ok?"

I am scared I feel as if I am crushed between two walls."

Joy's eyes were badly bruised and swollen her face was bandaged just as her arms and legs. "I can't move or open my eyes. What has happened to me? Where is my family?"

"Don't try to move too suddenly, you are just feeling fatigued and sore. You were in a coma for 3 weeks. I am Dr. Swartz. I was the doctor that operated on you after your accident."

"Wait... what?' Joy tried to move but she was sadly mistaken. She could barely wiggle her fingers. Her pain was minimal, but somehow she knew that her injuries were serious. It hurt for Joy to speak. Her forehead creased as she swallowed under her bandaged skull. Her throat felt as if she had swallowed glass. She began to gasp for air.

Dr. Swartz quickly dropped his clipboard onto the bedside table and fetched the cup of ice-cold water, and a straw. "Here Drink this."

Joy sipped slowly flinching as the cold water wet her palate. Even the cool liquid burned to her throat, it pan was different, as though sores on her tonsils were being burnt away.

"Slow," Dr. Swartz directed. "Take your time. Your throat is very sensitive as we just removed the tubes from your throat less than 48 hours ago. I can only imagine how thirsty you must be. I want to talk to you a bit about your case."

Joy slowly wiggled her fingers, indicating that she understood the Dr.'s words.

"Joy you were in a terrible car accident. Your car sped off the road and into the river just below the hill. It is a miracle that you are alive. The impact of the water broke the windshield of the car. You suffered some blow to your head. You slammed into the steering wheel of the automobile, which caused some neurological damage, to your optic nerve."

"What are you saying?"

"More simply put, the occipital lobe is where sight is processed which comes from the cranial nerve II, the optic nerve," Dr. Swartz was using hand motions to convey his message. Feeling odd at the silence in the room, he realized that Joy was unable to see his hand gestures. Dr. Swartz called out to Joy to make sure she had not fallen to sleep as he explained his prognosis.

"Joy, your visual perception has been severely damaged. As I'm sure you are aware, that **Visual perception** is the ability to interpret information and surroundings from the effects of light reaching the eye." Dr. Swartz paused to try and get some form of response from Joy, indicating she understood his words.

"Wait! What is all this? Is there someone that can come and explain all this in English?"

Dr. Swartz pinched his lips and folded his arms, grateful of Joy's inability to witness his growing irritation. He was slightly aggravated having read Joy's file. Her level of intelligence was way above average.

Dr. Swartz placed a puzzling hand under his chin, and as if hit with compassion he softened his aggressive tone. Pulling the visitors chair up to the side of Joy's bed, he cleared his throat and began again. "Mrs. Anderson, due to the severity of your injury's your retina's were singed. Which means you may regain some of your sight but not all. Our team of Ophthalmologist's and I performed an extensive amount of tests to evaluate your sight.

The neurological damage in relation to the brain that allows for vision is severe. We have concluded that you are in fact, legally blind. I know this may be a lot to take in, but I need you to understand what type of life you will lead after sustaining such an injury."

Joy began to black out. None of what the doctor was saying made any sense. She could not recall the moments leading or following the accident. She had no interest in discussing them either. She wanted to know where her family was.

"Excuse me. I don't mean to interrupt." Joy tried to clear her raspy voice unsuccessfully. "I don't understand. Will I regain my sight?"

"We are not sure Mrs. Anderson. Many people diagnosed with blindness, have experienced periods where they can see clear as day, as if they were never blind. Others see light, shadows, or just can't see in color. We are however optimistic about your situation. You have surpassed all of our expectations."

"Where is my family? "

"Your husband is out with your children waiting for the results of my evaluation. I did not tell your husband about your issue with sight. You just woke up and I did not want to overwhelm them with science and medical jargon. I wanted to talk with you to determine how lucid you were. I see that you are a literary agent and hold a degree in psychology yourself, so you understand the functions of the brain and mind.

However, being a victim of such tragic events can alter the most intelligent persons. I would like you to seek counseling. I would also like you to take the time to just recover, this means, NO WORK," Dr. Swartz tilted his glasses to get a better look at his patient. He could not tell by way of facial expression, her attitude towards the matter; but the silence spoke for itself.

"Joy, it will take you some time to get used to the new you; but I see no reason why you will not be able to continue in your life's work. You will just have to be patient. I am setting you up with some rehabilitation as your wounds heal. "

"I understand." Joy commented without emotion or the slightest interest to continue the conversation. "This is some new me," Joy whispered sarcastically.

"Mrs. Anderson, with today's technology you can use the voice command system on your computer to write, and correspond with your clients. You will be fine. The rehab will help you learn how to live with your disability. Many learn to read within a year. I have great confidence in you. I will leave you now to visit with your family. I am sure they are very anxious to speak with you."

"Wait! Joy took all that she could muster to get the docs attention before he whisked out of the room. Please… do not tell my family about my blindness. I don't want them to know."

"I wouldn't advise you to be silent in a matter as serious as this. You will need all the support you can get."

"I understand, but if I am going to live with this I need to deal with it in my own way. My family isn't used to my not being able to carry the world and tend to their needs. I think that they are devastated enough. I will tell them; but in my own way and on my own watch. Please just extend me this courtesy."

"I have no choice. It is against policy for me to divulge information without consent. I will, however advise you to tell your husband right away. It is important that he understands the extent of your injuries. He seems like a very good man. He hasn't left this hospital in the three weeks you have been here."

"Really…" Joy smiled and tried to adjust her position in bed. "Patrice is a Godsend," Joy spoke in an elevated gesture as the annoying twinge continued to aggravate her. Her narcotics must have shut off midsentence. She moaned at the flame of pain that flowed through her torn flesh and broken bones.

"Are you ok, Mrs. Anderson?"

"I think the meds just wore off."

"Ok, I will get a nurse to get you something for pain right away. In the meantime I will send in your family so that you can see them."

"Thank you." Joy was exhausted. She squinted because her eyelids were itching. She grimaced at the agony as she squeezed her eyes shut in an attempt to relieve the itchiness.

Dr. Swartz was gone in a flash. His long white jacket flew in the wind as the revolving door closed slowly. Just before the door clicked into its sill, she heard a familiar voice. It was Justin. She tried to pry her eyes open to test the severity of her injuries, but they were glued shut by crusted pus.

Joy began to panic. Her breathing grew rapid and her heart felt as if it were fluttering about in her chest. "What's happening to me she thought?" Trying to regain her composure she began to tell her self that things were going to be okay. The pain and loss of sight would just be temporary.

Joy was beginning to use her breathing technique to regain control of her mental capacity. Until, suddenly, a woman's voice uttered words of discouragement. They were so loud and clear she could have sworn the strange woman was standing just over her head.

"You are blind, you idiot. You will never see the faces of your husband and children again. Now look at you. Once again lost and taken into a vulnerable depressive state. Are you trying to kill me? I would just assume so."

"Hello!" Joy called out frightened by the woman's words of discouragement. Her pupils moved rapidly under her badly bruised eyelids. "Is anyone there? Who are you? What are you talking about?" Her presence was gone as quick as she came. She whispered into Joy's ear, leaving behind a cool breeze that frosted the tip of her nose. The sensation was an awakening of her sixth sense.

Joy heard her words, but quickly let them go. She was excited to see her family. Realizing that she would not be able to see their beautiful faces, a tear strolled down the sides of her eye. Her tears began to pour and soaked up by the gauze that covered the remainder of her face. They were quickly absorbed. Joy heard the door of her room open, and then the soft scuffs of little feet. She knew then that her boys were in the room. Lagging behind dragging was her daughter. "How frightened she must be," Joy thought to herself. She did not want any of her children to see her like this.

Justin stepped forward. She could smell him instantly. Again, the tears wet the dried pus on her eyes. Justin leaned in and touched her dry and cut lips. "I am so sorry," Justin whispered unable to hold back the emotion that had cut off his breathing. He began to sob hard like a baby and fell into the seat, next to Joy's bed. Joy wiggled her fingers, as she tried to reach for Justin's deep shining waves. She longed to touch is soft mane. She wanted to touch him, to comfort him.

It was not his fault as she led him often to believe. He was her muse, and the only one she knew would care enough to listen and take heed to her feelings. Burdened often with the dysfunctions of her family, she held her tongue.

Tired and frustrated with their obvious lack of respect for her, and her own livelihood she took out her anger on Justin often. It was a fight she had not planned. Her anger flowed from deep within her pores. She could not stop her mouth from moving and slaying his very being. She was so angry, so rude and horrifically nasty she herself could not believe it.

Memories prior to her accident started to flow as she calmed the worry from Justin's brow. She was guilty of tearing him to shreds because of her need for acceptance now she could hardly stand the feel of her own skin.

Her mother showed up at her place of business after years of very little contact to ask her for help. Joy's mind scattered angrily, but still in need of the comfort and closeness a daughter longs to have with her mother, she let go of the past. Gullible Joy fell for her Mother's plea and gave her five thousand dollars from their joint account.

Justin was furious when he found out. It was not the money he kept stating to a confused belligerent Joy It was the fact that she had kept it from him and lied when the bank statement rang true of her deception. Joy grabbed for her purse and threatened to leave him as she always did, when she did not have the answers or when conflict arose.

Justin called her bluff, an unusual stance from his normal reaction to Joy's threats. He tossed Joy, her keys and blew her a kiss goodbye sarcastically as he knew her better than anyone. Joy shook her thoughts back into reality and managed to abandon her thoughts of guilt.

"It's Okay." Joy finally managed to speak. She did not want Justin to feel responsible for her accident. It was neither one of their faults. A driver was careless and lost control.

Joy called her attention to her children. The boys were afraid and stayed towards the back of the room. Joy could feel the tension. She could not see them, but she could hear Jr. asking Ashley if it were their mother under the bandages. He thought that perhaps she was a mummy or ghost.

"Shh!" Ashley whispered loudly, pulling Jr. close by her side. She jerked him so hard. Joy could hear him grunt and his shoes scuff the tile floor.

"Don't pull on your brother like that Ash," Joy scolded. "Come to mommy. The three of you, come here. I need to tell you all something."

Ashley and the two boys inched slowly towards Joy's bed. Justin gathered himself and picked up his head from his slumped stance. Justin encouraged them to come closer to their mother. Jr. took his small hand and placed it on Joy's swollen fingers.

"Mom!" he yelled "You in there? What happened to you?"

"Mommy had a little accident, but I am going to be alright. I am glad you are here. Where is your little brother?"

"Right here, open your eyes!"

Justin looked up and took hold of Jr. He placed his hand on the small of his back and began to coach Justin Jr., about his mother's condition. "Son she can't open her eyes right now. They are sore, and bruised. Its better if she keeps them closed."

Ashley was quiet. She didn't know what to say and she was afraid to come any closer to her mother. Worried that her mother would be angry or sad that she refused engage in the visit, she forced herself to ask her mother if she was in any pain. "Mom, I hope you feel better. Are you in any pain? I could get the nurse." Ashley felt so uncomfortable she would have given anything to get out of the room. Joy could sense that she wasn't interested in staying in the room, but decided that she couldn't give her a pass.

Her presence made her feel alive and she needed her children to be close.

"No honey, I feel as good as can be expected. It looks much worse than it is. I can't see you, but I can tell that you are far away. Could you come closer? Your voice is a mere echo. Why are you so distant?"

"Mom you know I hate hospitals. I hate being here. I hate that you are here. Dad can we go, please…"

Justin looked up with a look on his face that could have killed. Ashley stifled herself abruptly.

"What's wrong?" Joy said softly. Her throat was hurting and her arms and legs felt crushed. She didn't want to alarm Justin and the kids, so she pushed the nurse call button discreetly. Justin noticed how quiet Joy had become and that her nurse call button was on.

"Are you ok Joy?"

"Yes, fine."

"Babe, it's me you are talking to. If there is something I can do I would like to know?"

"Just a little pain that's all. I alerted the nurse. The doctor said that he was going to let the nurse know that I needed some medication for my pain, but she has yet to come."

"How long ago was that Joy?"

"Justin its ok, calm down. The pain just got a little worse. I went ahead and sounded my alarm to remind the nurse's station is all. Please calm down. I don't want you to get all worked up for nothing. You should take the kids home. I am sure they have had a long day. I don't want them to see me like this for too long. Besides the boys could have nightmares. I don't want them to get this image of me locked into their minds."

Joy tried to smile but the sores on her lips cracked and started to bleed. She licked her wounds and could taste the salted blood. Justin grabbed for a napkin and wiped her lips softly.

"Justin," Joy said softly.

"What is it?"

"My lips hurt like hell."

Justin fiddled around in the drawers next to the bed and retrieved the complimentary chap-stick from the top drawer, to soothe the burn of his wife's torn lips.

Joy was filled with a soothing sensation a mist the pain, as her husband touched her lips. Joy smiled, "So, how bad do I look? I mean from what you can see. My face feels so swollen under these bandages. What if I don't look the same? What if my face is deformed or scarred?"

"All that doesn't matter, I love you. The important thing is that you are alive. I want you to concentrate on getting better, so that you can come home, Ok?"

"Ok." Joy was weak with pain. The pain had become so

unbearable she was nearing her breaking point. She wanted badly to call out for help, but she didn't want to alarm her children. "J…," Joy paused as the pain stifled her breathing. "Please take the kids home. I need to get some rest."

Justin could take a hint. He could tell that Joy was in pain and didn't want the kids to bear witness to her suffering. "Ok babe, we are going to go home. Get some rest." Justin coached the kids to come close to their mother and say good- bye. They each gave her a kiss on her lips. Jr. was playing with his mother's fingers. He didn't want to leave. He was very protective of his mother.

"Jr., it is time to go. We will come back and visit mom soon." Jr. stood his ground for a moment later. He retreated when Justin lowered his eyes. Jr. knew he had better do what he was told. Ashley came close to her mother and kissed her softly. She whispered I love you and ran from the room. She was on the verge of tears, and in her preteen year's it was against the rules to show signs of emotion.

Justin looked down at Joy one last time before grabbing up the boys and retreating from the room. "I love you babe, he whispered as he opened the door to leave. Coming into the room was the nurse, bearing the gift of narcotics.

"It's about time." Justin scolded. He couldn't help himself. It angered him that the doctors and nurses weren't taking care of Joy. He looked back at Joy smiled and jolted down the hallway to get Ashley.

Joy's veins warmed as the medicine seeped into her blood stream. In mere moment's her mind drifted and asleep she went. Numb to the pain, but hurt for her family, as she so longed to be with them.

~2~

HOME SWEET HOME

The next two weeks of rehab went by in a blur. Joy recovered from most of her injuries with flying colors. Her sight was the most disabling issue from the accident. Joy blew a frustrated hand gesture towards the nurse asking her to perform a few more leg lifts. "I know you mean well but I'm pooped. I just want to walk without a cane, maybe run a few laps around my living room and kitchen. I need to keep up with my two little rug rats. I am in no way interested in running a marathon, Nurse Betty.

"You could have fooled me," Nurse Betty chuckled. "You have been G.I. Jane to most of the nurses in this wing. I am motivated to get on a treadmill myself for a spell."

Joy laughed hard. As she wiped the sweat from her arms and neck. Opening her drawers to retrieve her belongings she froze as if lost in time, and smiled for just a moment. She loved the sound and the way it felt to have some normality and happiness in her life. She was so excited about her recovery. The nursing staff showed very little concern for her recovery, except for Nurse

Betty.

Nurse Betty always pushed her to fight just a little harder. Joy grew quiet as her mind drifted. Leaving the hospital after such a long stay was frightful. She was filled with mixed emotion. She found herself becoming quite teary eyed as she continued to pack the remainder of her things.

"Joy, it's ok? You will be fine." Nurse Betty comforted, as she too felt the lump settling in her throat. "I am going to leave you to get the rest of your things in order. Justin already phoned. He and the kids are on their way to pick you up."

Joy managed to smile through her confused state. "Ok Thanks. I will be ready shortly."

Joy squeezed her eyes tight before she made an attempt to open them. Her deep brown eyes lightened to a soft hazel after the accident. They blended perfectly with her cappuccino colored skin and natural spiral mane that danced just below the nap of her neck.

Joy opened her eyes greeted by a blinding white light. Literally, shocked by the painful blow, she shuddered at the thought of a second attempt to open her eyes. Taking in a deep breath she bravely opened her eyes for the second time slowly. Her vision was blurred. She could make out shadows at best. Everything was in black and white. She was now, a character in a 1950's drama. All she needed was a stick of ruby red lipstick and finger waves.

Joy closed her eyes and continued to pack her things. She had become quite used to the dark. She could feel when others were near and her sense of smell heightened. Joy became overwhelmed with fear when she thought about reuniting with her family. Her biggest hope in recovery was to regain her sight.

"Mrs. Anderson? Are you all set to go home today?" The discharge nurse on duty came by with her clipboard to run through her list, standard protocol for patients being discharged.

Joy laughed to herself at how serious the nurse sounded. She was quite interested in what she thought she could steal from the hospital, some towels, a gown, maybe some slipper socks. She sure as hell didn't want the watered down lotion and shampoo. Joy smirked and let out a loud chuckle at her thoughts, "Now, Dove and Caress, is cause for worry," she spoke with an arched eyebrow while gathering her belongings from the side table drawers.

"Yes I am quite excited. A bit worried, but I am very excited to see my family." Joy looked down when she realized that she wasn't going to be able to see anyone, not the same anyway She had in fact been dreading going home. She was going to be faced with yet another challenge. She was fearful of going back to her life as a mother, let alone her business.

The voice command program she had set-up on her laptop was an intelligent invention. However it had quite a few quirks to work out. Most of her dictation was poorly imputed. The playback was both hilarious and illiterate. She would be sure to forfeit her license if she published works relying on the good sense of her computer alone.

"Don't worry about it Joy. Your family is ready and waiting for you to come home. The kids are very excited. Justin was telling the staff how much they were doing to help you get settled in. The kids are making you a welcome home dinner and cleaning the entire house for you. What a treat? I wish my kids would volunteer to do the laundry, take out the trash maybe wash a dish or two."

"Oh Girl don't worry." Joy chuckled as she stood slowly to put her things in her bag. "This is all just temporary. They will be back to their normal destructive selves the moment they get wind I can scramble an egg. I will be sure to milk this for what its worth. I'll have an update for you by the time my next check-up rolls around." Joy turned towards the air blowing in slightly through her 5th floor window. "The air feels good." Joy smiled at the thought of the wind blowing into her hair.

"Good Luck to you." The discharge nurse scratched on her board and left with a satisfactory spin.

"Yea Thanks." Joy reached down to retrieve her bag. She heard the door opening her heart skipped a beat, "Justin is that you?"

"No, just me, I just wanted to make sure I said good bye

before I left for the day. You know I'm happy you are better, but sure sad to see you go. I am going to miss our late night chats. It made my nights go by fast. Oh and the laughs. Thanks for listening to my ranting about the other nurses. This wing has some rather funny characters. I often wonder where they got their credentials."

"You will be surprised." Joy laughed. "I will miss you too."

"I know you are worried about regaining your eye sight. There are plenty of success stories that you can derive some motivation from. You may only be able to make out shadows for now, but who knows in a year's time. If you continue your rehabilitation you may make a full recovery. Don't always listen to what these doctors say. You and I both know that there is a higher power working in our favor."

"Yes. I know Betty thanks. Sometimes I have to be reminded about God and his grace and mercy.   Even though he is always showing us his goodness, we forget about the blessings he has bestowed upon us. I will take this one day at a time." Joy zipped her bag and sat on the edge of the bed. Her lunch had arrived. She could smell the chicken and potatoes.

"Well eat your lunch. Justin and the kids should be here any minute. I wouldn't want him to tear the place down if he found out we didn't feed you."

Joy smiled, "Who Justin?" Joy commented sarcastically as if she didn't know her husband could cause a stir.

"Yeah, Him," Nurse Betty sashayed from the room leaving Joy to enjoy the comforts of peace and solidarity for one last time. She was soon to be greeted by a tribe of overly excited children and a husband that would drive her crazy with questions and pampering. Not that she minded it much.

ONE YEAR LATER

~3~

MRS. JOY ANDERSON

"Honey, do you have everything you need?"

"Yea, I think so. I wish you were coming with me."

"I know sweetie, but you will be fine. Just give your Father a chance. He and his Family are very excited to meet you. You have a grandmother and grandfather you've never met. Many people should be so lucky to have two sets of living grandparents." Joy looked down at Ashley's floral printed bed spread. Her mind drifted away to a far away land. "Ever since my Father died, I've seen things a lot differently. I know Justin has been your Father since you were 2 years old, but you should know your biological Father as well. Justin and I have had our disagreements about this from time to time. However, we both agreed that up until now, you were too young to be bounced around. We just wanted to protect you. So please don't blame your Father, he has made a number of mistakes. Although I can't say that he doesn't love you. He does so very much, both of your Fathers."

"Mom all that is well and good and I know that you guys were protecting me. That's what parents do. I get it. I also get that I have a Father. I don't care about visiting those people. If they knew about me, and where we lived, why haven't they come to see me? I don't want to go?"

"You're going!"

"Why? What is this really about Mom? Is this because of the house, and the stress you have been under? I can help. I know the boys can be a handful."

"No Ash, you don't have to. I want you to go and enjoy yourself. I need you to. It's not the house, it's me."

"Are you sick? Ashley began to get worried. She started to shake immediately, as the tears began to stream down her face. She always had a hard time with stress and anxiety. It was as if she went into panic mood at the slightest notion that something was wrong.

"No!" Joy smiled crookedly as her lips quivered visibly. She was lying and she couldn't hide the emotional effects that stormed upon her. She hated lying to her Family about her recent battle with illness. Her physical health was deteriorating. As a result, her mental state of mind was flawed. She became delirious at times, with a vicious rage that she could not explain. Her actions were murderous. Her memory was short, just as her temper. The Family knew as much. The tension so thick, often you could cut it with a knife.

Justin was close to breaking down himself. She thought for sure he'd file for divorce. Joy couldn't bring herself to tell the family that she was dying. She knew Justin well. He and the children would waste the time she had left pitying her. Sending them away while she went through treatment was best.

Joy and her sister Samantha spent countless hours researching possible treatment centers and trial studies, for her rare lung disease. Ever since the doctor called with the news Joy was on edge. Sam begged Joy to just tell her Family what was going on so that they could support her. Her change in mood was obviously unsettling to the children, because she was usually such a fun loving, easy going spirit, a workaholic but clearly devoted to her family.

Sam and Joy did stumble upon a small research project that involved some heavy duty consent forms and cash. Joy didn't care she had to try something before giving in to informing her Family of the news. The treatment would cost $10,000. Ten thousand, Joy couldn't afford at the time. Justin and Joy had just bought a home. Her business loan was excessive, and tutoring for Ashley was an arm and leg. Although Justin's business flourished she couldn't go to him for the money, without explaining the need for such a large amount of cash. So she was forced to take her business elsewhere, a place where she'd rather not expose. It was almost as bad as going to a loan shark for the money.

Darin, Joy's Ex, supplied the funds. His cocky throwback swag was from something out of the old gangster film, "New Jack City." He sat at the head of the table unnecessarily far from reach, as he discussed the terms of the loan. Joy nearly threw up as he whistled with his teeth and his tongue. He always wore this nasty, gritty, sex face, when he talked to her. His nose was turned up and his brow creased as if something smelled.

Joy knew the game already she knew exactly what he wanted. In exchange she would finally agree to send Ashley down to visit for a few months. Joy swallowed hard as she agreed. She didn't have an excuse not to send her since her preteen years arrived. Her main excuse had always been that Ashley was much too young to be traveling alone, or visiting strangers without her presence.

"Mom, are you ok?"

"What I'm fine? I just drifted off for a moment."

"Yea, I know. You were squeezing my hand. Is everything ok?

"Yes of course. I'm just going to miss you, is all…"

"I am too. That's why I should stay home." Ashley cheesed with her bright overly exaggerated smile, she used when she were trying to get her way.

"Nice try! Grab your things the train is always early when

we are running late."

"Mom, you always do that."

"Yea, but this time you really have a train to catch. So let's go. Let's go." Joy threw her hands in the air shooing Ashley to grab her bags.

Justin was already heading for the car with the boys in tow.

"Hey were you going to say goodbye?"

Justin turned around with a glare in his eyes that burned Joy's face. She could literally feel the heat as she touched her reddening cheeks.

"I wasn't aware you cared, with the way you are shoo flying us about the house. One would think you were deliberately trying to get rid of us for some odd reason."

"Justin stop, you are being ridiculous. I am going on my book tour. I have a ton of research to do, meetings…" Joy shook her head and raised her arms, as she pinched her lips tightly together. "This trip will be good for you and the boys. I will drive up next week. It makes no sense to postpone the trip, waiting around for me. Go! Take the boy's they are going to love the snow." Joy smiled and bit her bottom lip at Justin seductively.

"Whatever Joy," Justin couldn't help but smile at his lover and best friend.

"I just wish you would put this book tour aside. You can go and sign books anytime."

Joy looked down at the ground solemnly and kicked a few pebbles from her garden back into its bed. Realizing that she may be giving away the possibility that something was in fact wrong, she perked up as if a switch was turned on and off. "Yea you say that now; but when the publishing company refuses to pay my advance, you will be singing an entirely different tune."

"Funny Joy, real cute, you better have your ass in Yellow Brook by noon Sunday morning. Remember we are taking the boys for their Jr., ski lesson."

"Ok, Big Daddy. I will be there with bells on. I can't wait for you to see my night in the snow lingerie."

"Yea me either." Justin grinned. "I doubt you'll be wearing it long. Justin winked at Joy and got into the car. The boys were fastened tightly in their seats and screaming, "Daddy let's go." They were anxious to get on the road. "I love you Joy." Justin screamed out the window as he began to back out of the drive way.

"Oh Yea," Joy replied smiling generously. "For how long, just for today?"

"No Babe, *Always Infinitely.*"

Joy waved her last goodbye and ran into the home to recover, from the cold on her bare soles. She slammed the front door and ran to her soft shaggy rug to warm her chilling feet. "Wow, I'm really going to do this. What If it doesn't work?" Joy blew a tendril from her eye. It was itching and irritating her eyebrow. She plopped down on the couch and sighed. "I hate that I lied about this whole treatment business; but I just couldn't bear to get Justin's hopes up. I hadn't even told him I was sick, and if he thought there were some chance at a cure he would be sure to stress himself. I couldn't risk him worrying about me. We have the kids to worry about. I do hope this works." Joy was pacing the living room floor, until she found herself in the kitchen searching for her Hagen Daz Ice cream, and a huge spoon. "I hope and pray I can just make this nightmare go away." Joy said as she gulped down a huge spoon full of ice cream and looked into her reflection peering through the spoon.

Joy gathered her thoughts and took the tour around her home. She hadn't been home alone in such a long time. She didn't know what she was going to do with herself. Joy locked the doors and windows of her home, and made her way to the upstairs bedroom. She had a plan to soak in the tub and review a couple of chapters, of her life's work before going to bed. She was shaky about how her book would end. So she decided to use her time soaking in a tub of bubbles to perhaps brainstorm some fresh ideas.

Joy couldn't help but think of Justin and the kids. Ashley should have been half way to Los Angeles by now. Joy thought to give them a couple more hours before she phoned to check on them.

As the water filled the tub, Joy's mind raced. She really had no interest in reviewing her notes on the book. Her stomach was hurting. She felt nervous and uneasy. Stress and anxiety were two of Joy's major setbacks that threatened her sanity. She wasn't comfortable being alone in the home. Nor had she been away from her children or Justin longer than a day at work, or temporary stay, at the hospital, since the accident. The home was too quiet and dark.

Joy turned off the water to her bath, and ventured off into her master suite, to let the water cool before she took a dip. She had her own, "cleansing system" she liked to call it. She would run the bath as hot as the temperature allowed, and wait for the water to cool to her liking. Lightly skipping about the room, Joy located her remote and flipped through the channels. As she turned she noticed that all the channels were blue. "Damn It," An irritated Joy threw her arms in the air and rolled her eyes. Blowing her hair from her brow she smacked the side of the television. "I hate this TV. I knew we should've switched services." Joy shut off the receiver and hit the power button to reset the device. As she waited for the television to reset, she scurried into the bathroom to check her bath.

As Joy tipped into the bathroom, the winds blew wildly rattling the glass and shudders. Joy's stomach dropped but she quickly gained composure. She leaned over the tubs edge to check the temperature of her bath, when suddenly, the glass window of

~ 33 ~

the bathroom shattered, falling inches from her head. More than shaken, Joy ran from the bathroom to search for her tennis shoes and gun. She thought for sure there was an intruder afoot. Boldly shuffling through her drawers and boxes, she cursed Justin and thanked him just the same. The gun was a plus in this particular situation, however to find it she was sure as dead.

Justin thought it best to protect themselves and their property. The neighborhood was very nice and quiet, however his motto was, "Better safe than sorry." Justin bought his and her guns in case of an emergency. Joy sighed as she grabbed her 22 and unhooked the safety. She moved quickly to the hidden door of her bedroom closet.

The bedroom closet led to the basement. It was the perfect hideaway in case of an emergency. Joy grabbed her purse and cell phone, as she ran down the stairway towards the basement. She quickly powered on her phone and dialed 911, as she bolted the trap door.

"911, what is your emergency?"

"I think someone is trying to break into my home," Joy's heart beat fast and her blood pressure elevated from the adrenaline pumping in her veins.

"Ma'am, get to a safe place. There is a terrible storm coming, she is the most horrific our parts have seen. The Reports from the Natural Disaster Bureau predict her to touch ground in approximately ten minutes."

"Oh My God," Joys mind drifted. Her thoughts ran together and showed flashes of her life, as though they were scenes from an old movie.

"Ma'am...did you see the intruder?"

"No, the window broke in my bathroom. I thought someone was trying to get in."

"Get to a safe place. It may have just been the winds from the storm. It's coming down pretty hard out there."

Joy swallowed hard, as the worry began to burn her cheeks and ears. Her skin was incredibly hot and her stomach felt sick. "I am in a safe place," Joy mumbled as it was becoming hard for her to speak. "I locked myself in the basement."

"Good Ma'am. Stay put."

Joy was delirious. Her thoughts ran wild. She couldn't help but think about her family. She wondered incessantly, wondering, if they had traveled out of range of the storm, dodging the horrible twister.

"Ma'am..."

Joy was standing with the phone glued to her ear. Hanging up the phone, she quickly switched her psyche into survival mode and hung up, and called her attention to the beeping sounds from her television. The emergency broadcast system had just chimed in, protocol for natural disasters and safety guidelines were unconceivable. Joy listened and stood so still it was as though she were paralyzed. Her mind locked somewhere between la, la land and earth. She had completely blacked out just as quick, as her natural instincts rang. She couldn't hear or see a thing.

Joy was filled with odd feelings. She was nervous. Quickly, as if being pulled by a force outside her grasp of understanding. Joy searched the basement pantry for safety equipment and emergency supplies, another one of Justin's plans of action. He was serious about emergency procedures. He had the kids practice fire drills and earthquake precautions monthly.

As Joy rumbled around the pantry gathering supplies, she felt an enormous amount of fear hovering over her clouded mind. She had been in many storms, but none as gruesome as a tornado. Trying to get her water supply into the deep freezer, she winced with pain, as she tried to hike the 5 gallon jug of life just over the freezers edge. Just as she was able to get the jug into the freezer, the lights went out. "Shh…! That's just great." Joy slapped her hands on the side of her jeans and sunk to the floor just in front of the freezer. She buried her head in her hands and began to sob softly.

~**4**~

PRINCESS ASH

Ashley, stared blankly into the window of the train, as the country hills blew by. Passing through the San Joaquin Valley was peaceful and a great time to think things through. She was only twelve, but an old soul, much like her Father. Ash was nervous about meeting him. She didn't quite know how she was going to address the situation.

She wasn't exactly honest about her feelings. She wanted to get to know him and her new sister. She was just worried about hurting her Step Father's feelings. She knew her Mother wanted her to get along with both sets of parents. She expressed how lucky she was to be blessed with such a loving and accepting Family, often.

Although Ashley was excited about seeing her biological Father, she still had a number of questions she needed to have answered. As a new thought lit the memory bank in her mind, she looked down at her paper of scribbled pros and cons to jot down some of her most recent thoughts. She was very much like her mother. The pen and pad were her most treasured tools. They were also the most powerful. Ashley was great with creative writing, and had received a number of awards for her writing.

Deep in thought Ashley began journaling, the exciting adventures of her trip home. She called the adventure, "Home," because she was traveling to a place where she would meet the other half of her creator. Finally, the pieces of her soul would be united and she would be able to fully understand who she was, and where she had come from. She wrote of her past meetings with her Father. They were vague, but she remembered bits and pieces of their encounters. It was important to her to write, the description of him as she remembered. She wanted to fill in the blanks, when she saw him again.

Ashley was beginning to get sleepy. The Hot Chocolate was a Godsend. It calmed her nerves, and enabled her to write freely; but it relaxed her muscles so much she felt extremely exhausted. Suddenly, the lights went out overhead and the train shook violently.

Ashley unbuckled herself to get a better look at what was happening. She flew from her seat. Concerned, and out of touch with the seriousness of the situation, She swayed with trains vibration sliding from seat to seat as the train danced on and off the tracks.

A woman was slumped over in her seat and bleeding. She

was sitting next to a small girl who was in tears and screaming. Ashley was shaken herself. She rushed to help her sit up in her seat, and grabbed for a pillow. The woman was unconscious and the little girl seemed to be crushed by the seatbelt buckle lodged in her bulky parka. Ashley tugged at her belt to loosen the girl's belt and adjust the woman seated next to her in an upright position.

"You are going to be ok, is this your mother?" Ashley consoled the little girl whose eyes were beginning to well with tears.

"Yes," the little girl responded filled with fear and uncertainty. Her mother warned her about strangers but she felt safe speaking to Ash.

Ashley rubbed the girls arm and gave her a reassuring smile. "Sit tight, and keep an eye on your mom, ok."

The little girl nodded to confirm she understood Ashley's instructions just before the trains lights began to flash on and off.

Ashley made her way back to her assigned seat as the attendants flowed through the aisles to help passengers stay calm. There was a loud chatter thundering down the small wing of train cars. Ash began to get alarmed. She reached for her phone but it had fallen from her coat pocket and on to the floor of the train. She caught sight of it just before it slid across the floor as she plopped back into her seat. Ash grabbed for her journal but, her gloves were too thick for her fingers to grab hold of the flimsy pages. The

Journal soared across the train car as the beverage cart flew past her cheek. She could feel the burn, as it scratched her, much like the rug burns, her older cousins gave her at family functions.

Ashley began to panic fumbling about her seat she grabbed for her seatbelt as the train began to sway out of control. Her hands were shaking so badly that she could hardly buckle herself in. The bell rang just above Ashley's head as she grabbed for her armrests. Her heart was beating out of her chest.

"Ladies and Gentlemen, please get to your seats and take refuge."

"Refuge…?" Ashley whispered to herself. "Could we use 12 year old language here? What the Fuck is going on?" Ashley quickly stifled herself, as she could hear her mother's voice in her head telling her to remain calm, and watch the language. Ashley swallowed hard as the panic button resounded just over head. The Conductor mumbled on incoherently. All she could hear were muffled sounds of panic and distress. It was in that moment Ashley let go of her cocky attitude, and prayed that her Mom and Dad would come to her rescue.

Ash closed her eyes tightly as the loud sounds of wind and rain hit against the metal of the train. The trains Plexiglas windows shattered, and the body of the train melted into thin air. Ashley felt lifted into the heavens as the wind whipped her and the other passengers in her car up into the air. The spinning made her nauseous. She hated rollercoaster's. Wind and dust entered her lungs as her napkin mask, she held tight around her nose and mouth ripped from her face. She never opened her eyes. She dreamed as if she were a ballerina dancing at an opera. She was without fear gliding upon the stage. She was gone without a trace, a peaceful trip that she happened to chance upon.

~5~

NO EXCEPTIONS

"This trip is long over-due boys." Justin ranted on, as he drove up the winding hills. The sky had turned dark and the winds blew furiously. Traffic was so backed up he could see lines of cars for what seemed like miles ahead. "Hold on Boys, I am going to see what the hold-up is, around here." Justin jolted with a dash as he jumped from his truck to take a look at the scene. The wind was cold and chilling to his bones, his muscle tee blew in the wind like a sheer scarf.

Justin thought about his coat that was in the trunk section of his Suburban and ran against the wind to grab it. As the winds velocity began to pick up, Justin threw on his coat anxiously in an attempt to shield himself from the blows of the wind and rain.

As the showers began to pour, he took notice to the other drivers looking high towards the east of them. A large cloud was swirling in place, and growing larger by the second. Justin ran towards his car, after slamming the trunk of his Suburban.

"Boy's!" Justin screamed afraid more than ever. The Boys were sleeping soundly. The sounds of rain patted the windows of the truck, rocking the boys to sleep. Justin's eyes began to swell with tears. Others around slowly got into their cars to take cover. Some stood and embraced their loved ones bravely to face the inevitable.

Justin was lost in thought and in emotion. He was scared for the lives of his children. Joy was at home alone, he couldn't bear to think of the thoughts running through her mind. Justin's breathing grew shallow in his over-sized puff coat. He pulled himself from under the smothering fabric, and began to pray.

Frightfully, he grabbed for his steering wheel and locked eyes on his two boys sleeping in the back seat. Tears began to stream down his cheeks. Unable to tear his gaze from his children, he buckled his seatbelt slowly. Justin commanded his On Star to phone Joy. He was worried about her and wanted to make sure she was ok. The phone rang once and went straight to voice mail. Justin was so disappointed he wanted to break down and cry.

Clearing his voice he waited for the sound of the beep. "Joy, honey its Justin. I just wanted to check in on you. I love you, Honey. Talk to you soon." Justin knew in his heart that it may be the last call he would place. He was saddened at the thought that he wasn't with Joy during this disastrous time.

The last thing he wanted her to know was that he loved her. As he hung up the phone, via his blue tooth he removed it from his ear. It was coming down pretty hard. The other drivers were beginning to panic. Noticing the winds picking up speed and velocity he took notice to lock the doors and make sure all the windows were up in his Suburban.

As the spiraling Queen of winds sang, Justin curled tight in the backseat with his two boys shielding them from the possibility of broken glass.

The howling wind danced, to her tune of destruction as she captured the lives of men, women, and children; all looking with shocked helpless eyes, as there were no exceptions. After the winds treacherous vengeance on Mother Nature the roads were left with a soft whistle. Debris scattered the roads, bodies of all kind lay badly battered and bruised. The rings in their ears were the last sounds of life.

Justin closed his eyes as his shelter was swallowed into the wind. He went peacefully at the thought of his children dreaming serenely in the fold of his arms.

~6~

AFTER THE STORM

Joy came from under her wooden shelter. The whistle of the wind dissipated scampering behind was a soft whisper. Joy was so afraid she had never experienced such an event. When the tornado hit it was like the wind was screaming. The blustery weather was calling out murderous vengeance against the wrongs humans did upon their natural resources. She was stunned at the damage the tornado left behind. She was underground and still felt its wrath.

Joy winced as she pulled herself up from under the wreckage. Her wooden shelter gave way about half way through the storm. She was lucky to have recovered without medical attention, after suffering such a blow to the head.

During the storm, a can of half empty paint, fell from the edge of one of the wooden storage shelves above her haven; and hit her in the head.

Joy's arm however, was in worse shape. It had suffered the

blunt of the shelves demise. She used her shoulder to shield herself, as she was knocked to ground. After the blow to the head all the strength she could muster was to simply, ball up into the fetal position. Leaving her arm fully exposed her head and face protected.

Joy was crushed by the wood. With her arm in such pain it took some time to free herself. Joy threw herself into survival mode and limped from the wooden pile. She couldn't believe her eyes. The glass of the basement windows was broken and the curtains blew slightly as if breathing faintly. There was a shadow of light that streamed into the basement exposing some of the damage that lay upon the basement floor.

Joy stood in the middle of the lighted path and gazed out the window. She was slightly hunched over. The pain was excruciating. It was starting to cloud her judgment. For a moment she could have sworn she saw her husband Justin, standing just outside among the fallen debris, holding the hands of their three children.

Joy blinked anxiously trying to clear her mind and vision, as the warm blood from her battered head, dripped into her right eye. She hadn't realized she was bleeding. Joy frantically wiped the blood from her eye and forehead and blinked again limping towards the window as fast as she could. She nearly stumbled over her own feet, as her mind was moving faster than her body could carry her. She blinked again and grabbed hold to the windows edge. The glass from the shattered window pierced the raw flesh of her hands. She didn't take notice.

"Justin….Ash… Jr., Josh," she called out to the winds. They were whispering something. All she could see clearly were the remnants of the rose bushes her and the kids planted, when she and Justin first bought their home.

The petals were scattered on the ground and along the cement path which led to the backyard. Joy could see clear through the fence that once separated her and her neighbors. It was destroyed and taken by the tornado. Joy called out to her children once more.

"Ashley Josh, are you ok? Can you hear me?" Still nothing but the dim whisper of the wind, she couldn't even hear a small cry for help. It was like the town had been abandoned and she was its only resident.

Joy looked down at her hands. She was squeezing the window sill so tightly she hadn't noticed the blood oozing from her pinched fingers.

"Oh my God," Joy realized that she was hurt and looked out the window for one last glance, before she sought medical treatment. There was nothing but the wind remorsefully praying its apologies.

Joy retreated from the window and went to look for her emergency backpack she managed to pack just before the storm hit. She had found the first aid kit, Justin purchased in case of a natural disaster. It was in perfect condition, never opened.

Justin was funny like that. Over protective and well prepared. It was almost as if he was waiting for his chance to cast for the next season of, "Survivor."

Joy remembered how she used to tease him about his, "MacGyver," concoctions. He was always inventing some type of gadget out of little to nothing, to either protect himself or use for survival. Now she loved that very trait about him. Some of the, "Go, Go Gadget," monstrosity's were high on her list to help find, food, and shelter.

"I don't think you planned on a tornado hitting good ole sunny California, did you baby?" Joy was smiling as she talked to herself. She was busy climbing her way back towards the entrance of the basement.

"I sure hope we have something left to climb out to," Joy sighed.

~7~

THE SHADOW

Joy thought about her relationship with Justin. They were more than lovers, they had become best friends. The Anderson pact was a vow to handle the decisions of home and family jointly. It was hard to believe that they had been together for almost ten years. With every season's passing their love grew stronger. Loosing Justin would be unimaginable.

The Anderson's had only bought their home a year ago. It was their first official purchase together. They had rented and financed cars separately, but they had never actually purchased something of long term that they shared name and title. After they finally decided to get married it became official. They were going to walk the walk and truly trust one another with their lives and the lives of their children.

Justin and Joy had both suffered from the trials and tribulations of a dysfunctional home and family. So they took their devotion to one another quite seriously. Joy had some stability after she was removed from her mother's care. However, she never got over trying to make sense of what had occurred in her youth. She was still trying to gain love and acceptance from both her Mother and Father.

On the other hand, her father was trying to gain forgiveness from her. He blamed himself for the abuse Joy suffered at the hands of her mother's new boyfriend, at the tender age of 6. It would take Joy years to reveal her abuse. She had suppressed the memories of her nightmares to survive the harsh realities of the world.

As if her mother choosing a man over her wasn't enough. During her years of adolescence the dreams began. She was tortured nightly by the visits of the, "**Shadow**." The "**Shadow**," was the name assigned to her assailant. He'd appear after dark, when the house was quiet. He grew tired of her mother and would venture to other parts of the home to seek comfort.

His ritual became frequent as he stood in the lighted path just outside her door. Standing there breathing, she could see his chest rise and fall. The smell of beer on his breath stung her eyes, as if he were standing just over her.

After the abuse became a ritual, Joy often awoke with unexplained scratches and bruises on her arms and legs. Cuts that were so deep it looked as if she were cut with a knife. It was clear the markings were from fingernails, hers to be exact. She was fighting to free herself from the man. *"**The Shadow**,"* a demonic plague, a horrific reality that began to invade her dreams salting her innocence.

****

Joy's mind drifted into a distant place. She sat on the staircase of the basement, reliving her demons. The counseling sessions after her accident had gone far beyond the scope of her expectations.

Depression came along for the ride when she was released from the hospital. Joy was argumentative in session, and often refused to participate in discussion. The truths that she would just as easily burry along with her were challenged and sought.

After weeks of pulling teeth Joy finally opened up, enough to share her story. She was nearing close to a break through; but for some reason she shut down when the dreams came back to life. It was like a force from the devil and his advocates that were insistently, trying to keep her in their realm. Once the dreams came so did the voices, she was just as bad as the Shadow's wrath. It was if she encouraged her demise. She as in the other woman that plagued her mind, a soul, both Joy and her Doctor debated upon existing. She was damaged goods. She'd spent the better half of her adolescent life hiding her dark side. She was taunted; when sparks of this revelation were revealed. There was someone else that lay dormant in the corners of Joy's mind.

~8~

MEET LILIAN ANDREW'S

I am the Angel of Night, the demon prince of conception. My gift is of vanguard invention. I can bring forth both good and evil for my mind controls both quarry and praise. Andras is my other half, a killer of men by way of conjuring magic. I am one that has many faces, I am hard to detect. Deception is my game. Malice is my true claim to fame.

"Joy would you like to talk about your childhood, the abuse to be exact."

Joy cleared her throat. There was never a good time, to speak of such horrific acts, acts that should never have happened to an innocent child. Her legs grew weak. Her throat began to burn. It was hard to swallow, as her mouth went suddenly dry. The palms of her hands shook, tipping over the glass of water she attempted to grab. Giving up on wetting her parched lungs, she adjusted herself on the couch and folded her arms, as if to comfort herself.

Joy's forehead began to fold and bead with sweat. She sat

very still, remotely focused on the black and white oak table that sat just in front of the couch. Dr. Zimmerman was nothing but a mere shadow, of light. Her only clue as to the good in him, as opposed to the dark shadows, that lurked in her consciousness. Joy swallowed hard as she began.

I was 17, when the dreams resurfaced. They originated when I was 12. I quickly suppressed them and continued living in darkness. My caramel complexion was bright and glowed in the sun. The outside seemed bright and anew. Just beneath the first layer of skin was meat, tainted and rotting. My soul was dark, and dismal. The joy of life was gone. My reflection was a distorted, mirror of broken glass.

I was only 6 when it happened. I remember like it was yesterday, the wind in the trees, the darkness, and quiet of the night. I could smell him from a mile away. My door was always left open at night in case I had a nightmare. However, the nightmares weren't happening in my sleep. There were living breathing, torturous moments of my childhood. I would just rather forget it ever happened. I'm not sure that it did. At least I don't remember much of the abuse. I don't reckon anyone would want to, unless they were planning some sort of revenge. 14 years old was my time of awakening. The dreams began. So did my bout with the troubling, "Teen Opera" of adolescence.

I was short, awkward, the times were changing, and I was

lagging behind. I decided that my hair would look grand in one of those jerry curls, television commercials were advertising. The hair do turned out to be a hair do gone wrong. I was so excited to get to school, to showcase my makeover, only to realize that my new style was the hot topic of last year's fashion trend.

8th grade happened to be the year of A-symmetrical haircuts, short one side long on the other. I still can't understand the concept of cutting one side of your hair short and leaving the other long. What if I wanted to where a ponytail. I don't know, it seemed like a good idea at the time, so I joined in. I have this need…this need to be different, but the same equivalently. I share what is meant to be sacred to us as individuals."

"Is this going anywhere?" Dr. Zimmerman purposely queried, trying to egg Joy on towards a break into her maladjusted past.

"I don't know you tell me. You're the professional. I don't have an identity. I still question my own judgment."

"Last time I checked you wanted to be me. A counselor that is, Brain Doc."

"I did until I found out that my head was much too screwed up to remotely assist in someone else's problems. My cup has been full since I can remember. My mind has always raced, raced in many directions. Maybe that's why I have never been able to decide on a for sure career. I am an unstable victim of circumstance. I think I could use that excuse for the rest of my days. Many say you shouldn't over use your sob stories for sympathy. However, it has worked for me. Why fix what is not broken? I have been broken so many times and in so many ways it really doesn't matter to me if I am evidentially readable. It hasn't caused too much of a set-back. Brains and Beauty has some advantage you know.

Honestly, the thoughts in my brow are often not of my own will. I act on emotion where this…invasion, acts on rage. I am plagued daily with thoughts of suicide simply to end my torment. Is this open and clean cut enough for you?"

"So what do you do? How do you deal with this invasive woman?"

"Whatever sounds good enough to believe? I have no defense against this inhabitant. She is my curse. One that I propose I have been punished with, in another life."

Dr. Zimmerman was not, satisfied with Joy's use of her alternate psychosis. He tapped his pencil on his pad to a beat thumping about in his head, again looking to aggravate Joy's alternate ego. "You seem to enjoy using this new found addition to your personality to fall upon when you have clearly made a slip in judgment. It must be nice. So, how long do you plan on keeping up this act?"

"What act? I'm serious about my new practice."

"I'm not talking about your writing."

"Is any of this supposed to go anywhere? What does this have to do with my dreams? There back. I haven't had one for about 4 years now. About the time, Darrin and I broke up. What do think this could mean? My relationships go to shit, when the Shadow returns. It doesn't help that more often than not all I can envision are the shadows of my life, the good and the bad. It's hard to decipher what is what. I get scared."

"We went over this. You need to get past the issues you have with your father. It's time to grow up. You have to be the adult in this. I know it's hard to swallow but it is what it is."

"That's rich. How in the hell and I supposed to get over the fact, that my father wasn't there to protect me when I needed him. He let that man molest me over and over again. He left my mother to be beaten while he went on his creative ventures. I hate him."

"I don't think this is at all true. I think that you were a child, left in a horrific situation, but you were taken by family and well taken care of might I add."

"Is that supposed to make everything better, Dr. Seuss I mean these riddles you are throwing at me are great. Sure wish this information was of some use to me."

"We are out of time. The good doctor has clients waiting, other clients with real issues."

Dr. Zimmerman was anxious to get rid of Joy he had a date

with some files that could be very insightful to the origin of Joy's mental state.

"I don't know what to do ok? I need help more meds something."

"No doctor in their right mind will give you a prescription." Dr. Zimmerman didn't want to prescribe Joy any more medications that would add on to her possible hallucinogenic traits. She appeared lucid, at the present time. He noted that her mind could possibly remain uncompromised in the absence of therapeutic drugs. He knew full well that he could not prevent her from seeking counsel elsewhere but, he would try and keep her within his practice as long as he could. He was so close it became evident that the dreams and flashes started when she started taking the drugs. Without the hefty side effects, Joy would be forced to deal with her inner demons.

"Just forget it. What was this anyway? We spend an hour rehashing my indifference. I reopen the secrets of Pandora's Box, every time I come to you. I leave feeling just as broken and confused as when I came in. What is this? None of my family seems to give a shit about what I am going through. Or whether they truly believe me, is still a mystery. Tell me what to do? I can't keep coming back here and leaving empty handed. It's not fair. This talking to you about nothing is exhausting. Things aren't going to change. I at least need the meds to calm me. Don't do this.

I need the medication."

"No you don't. You need to deal with your real issues. If you keep masking them with drugs you are going to lose everything. You are not alone, in this."

"Yes I am doc. Yes I am." Joy grabbed for her purse and slung it onto her shoulder violently. She was dangerously close to brushing the Doc's face, with her leather hobo. She secretly, pondered upon knocking his glasses from off his face. He looked so brave and bold. Not a care in the world. He held all the cards. Joy didn't want to play his games any longer. She needed a new way to get her hands on medical supplies. Her usual fight with prescription drugs wasn't as bad. Lately, it's all she seemed to care about.

Joy ran down the hall to make the elevator. She was angry. Her plans were falling apart. If she didn't have the meds to fall back on, there was no way she would ever get sleep. Her mood swings were erupting far less sporadic. She was shaky at best, and her work was suffering severely.

"I want out of this mess of a life." Joy sunk to the bottom of the floor of the elevator and threw her head into her hands. "I just can't take this anymore. I can't go home."

"You must. You have children."

"How did you get here? I don't want to hear any more of your stupid ideas about me. I'm sick, sick in the head, ok. I need professional help."

"No you don't. You are sick, but not in the head. If you weren't so busy, feeling sorry for yourself you may be able to accomplish something."

"Well I don't need you. It's not the first time someone has abandoned me. Even, I don't believe in me. I don't expect you to stay. Why are you here anyway? All the confessions you made about my so called evil spirit. I just love how you showed the doctor a thing or two. I can't even get my prescriptions filled."

"Begging for them sure wasn't going to get the job done. Maybe it is time for old Sammy, to come and plead your case. You should start using your resources. They sure haven't hesitated in using your services for the greater good, when they need something done."

"Maybe right now, I just want to get the hell out of here, before I have a nervous breakdown."

"Nervous breakdown," Lillian shook Joy's head in amazement of how co-operative her brain was working towards deceit. "That may not be such a bad idea. You are thinking a little more along my lines of deception."

****

Joy shook the thoughts, visions and haunting spirits, to cause her attention to the whereabouts of her Family. If she could manage to find her phone charger, she would be able to get some juice on her phone. She was saving her battery to call Darrin. She was sure Ashley should have made the station by now. Justin she knew would have taken refuge with the boys, if he had the foresight to do so, before the storm hit.

Recovering from her slighted loss of focus, she continued up the barricaded staircase to make way through to her home. She was nervous, but hoped for a miracle.

~9~

SAMANTHA, "SAM I AM"

Sam awoke from her nap confused and discombobulated. She was shocked that she could sleep through such a tragic event. The tornado passed through her calm streets like a hovering cloud. After it touched ground miles away it lifted like a plane taking off. The evening news showed spectators reporting their sightings of the great tornado and its wrath.

"Wow!" Sam chuckled as she threw back the covers on her bed. That was some nap. She was well rested after her long snooze. She was so exhausted, but couldn't get to sleep so she took a sleeping pill to help calm her nerves. She had slept so soundly, if the house had been air lifted into another state, she wouldn't have even known it.

Sam got up and scooted to the edge of the bed to find out just where the tornado had touched ground. She was laughing out loud at some of the idiots broadcasting how scared they were of the whirlwind torpedo; but stood dangerously close to its angry winds.

"It had to be one of us," she said to herself as she shook off her restless state, to regain full conscious awareness. Sam turned her attention to the news broadcast.

"Disaster has struck in our otherwise sunny state. California has never seen such a storm. The angry winds of the great tornado have past. All we have left are remnants of our homes and precious belongings. There are shelters opening in nearby cities. If you need shelter, please do not attempt to stay in your home. The foundation of your homes may be very unstable. After suffering such a storm there are several problematic issues that can cause further horrific fatalities.

The American Red Cross is asking that you be careful around electric wiring and gas stoves. There could be a leak somewhere in your home or business. The American Red Cross is also asking that if you are a Dr., Nurse, or Health Care Provider and you are not injured, please look to find a shelter to volunteer your services. The county hospital was hit hard. The local clinic is open and is being prepared for emergency patients only. Patients with minor injuries will have to be looked after in their local shelters."

Sam sat down and as she began to worry. "Oh my God, I hope everyone is okay.' I better find my phone."

Sam ran about the room tossing her covers and pillows here and there to uncover her buried phone. She was beginning to get nervous the way she did when she wasn't in control. Diving onto the floor to retrieve her phone as it toppled out from under the crumbled bedspread. She fell to the floor as if rescuing a live grenade.

Sam dialed Joy's number without looking and paced the floor impatiently. "Damn it, Joy pick-up the damn phone." Sam had begun to get frustrated with Joy and her stupid electronic devices. She prized herself on having the latest of everything known to man, in technology. Yet she failed to answer or respond to any of her messages.

"God I hope you are ok." Sam grabbed for her shoes and slung them onto her feet. For the last two years it was only her and her older sister, Joy left in the family. The others were gone, gone on to bigger and better things. Sam was both envious and angry with her siblings for abandoning one another. She was stuck on family and believed in strength in numbers. With six other brothers and sisters she was confident that if they had vowed to stick together, nothing could break them.

Sadly, there closeness is what ultimately caused a need for separation. The others were the reason for most of the disputes in the family. The ones they loved couldn't understand why they had to be so close. Why they called one another when the other was in trouble or in harm's way. Quite often they were teased individually by their companions about who would be called to rescue them from their burning eyes.

Joy was the peace maker. She believed in family and she held on for as long as she could. She tried to foster and nurture the importance of family and education. Some of them listened. Some felt as if to feel the burn, was the essence of life. Joy believed in risks and taking those that would amount to something. "Selfish endeavors would only end in defeat." She whispered those words every time one of lucky 7 got into trouble.

"The lucky 7," is what she called them. Lucky she said they were, lucky to have such a task force of support. Even in times of indifference, if there was a knock on the door which threatened to bring harm to one of their flock, there would be a wage of war. No questions asked.

Sam paused as she grabbed for her purse. The aftermath of the storm, showed reports of the damage done in the city Joy lived. Sam dropped her purse and keys to the floor when pictures of the city were flashed upon her large 64 inch flat screen. She was so shocked and dismayed that she couldn't move. Her legs felt like stone. She was frozen. Her hand covered her open mouth and her eyes were wide with surprise. Sam's thoughts were spinning out of control. She didn't know what to do next. She quickly grabbed for her purse and keys and headed for the door. Fumbling to get her jacket on her arms she dropped her phone onto the kitchen floor. It shattered as it hit the tile flooring. Her case was like magic. It finally did its job. Her phone remained in mint condition. The shell was now trash; but her battery could easily be put back into her phone without complication.

"Calm down Sam everything will be fine." Sam tried to calm her frantic spirit as she dove for the floor to pick up the pieces to her phone. Her arm was half way in her leather blazer and her hair was thrown towards her face blocking her view of the phone. "You have got to get a hold of yourself. Oh My God… the boys, Charles. I hope they weren't in the middle of the storm?"

Charles and her children worked and attended school in downtown San Francisco. He and Justin were in business together, and worked out of offices in Oakland Hills as well as the San Francisco Bay Area. Sam was anxious to get in touch with Charles. She knew he had meetings during the afternoon but had no idea where they were located.

Sam finished gathering the necessities for her trip and mapped out the quickest route to get to Joy. Since most of the roads would be closed she would have to go around. She could only imagine the traffic. She had no choice but to go and find out if she was ok. Oakland was hit the hardest. The number of causality's grew by the minute. Sam changed the battery in her phone and sprinted to her car. She wanted to try Charles one last time before she got on the road.

Sam got into her car quickly and followed her safety

precautions, before dialing Charles again. "Come on Charles pick up." Sam wanted...needed to hear his voice. Even though she knew now that Charles and the kids didn't feel the blunt of the storm, she needed to know that they were ok. The most Charles and the boys experienced were some heavy rains for about a half hour. Sam breathed in deeply and exhaled as she heard Charles clear his throat in an effort to say hello.

"Hey... Sam. You ok? I have been trying to call you for at least an hour now. My phone has been going in and out since the power outage."

"Oh my God... I am so happy to hear your voice." Sam sighed with a sense of relief. "I didn't realize the power went out where you were, as well."

"Yea it's out, in blocks all over the city. We are having some sort of rolling blackout. The tornado took out some power lines in Oakland, power lines which we all happen to share. I'm just happy to hear that you are okay. I checked with the boy's school already. They are fine. All the students were ushered into the auditorium. The principle is holding all of the students there until the parents arrive to pick them up."

"Okay great. I am so glad to hear that."

"Where are you?" Charles noticed the quieting winds hitting the phones receiver. "Are you outside?" Charles asked with a hint of aggravation in his voice. "What are you doing outside? I heard the highway patrol discouraging anyone without an immediate need, to stay inside. You aren't going where I think you're going, are you Sam?"

"I have to Charles. She is all alone. Her book tour was this week. The children and Justin left this morning. She has to be worried sick. Plus what if she's hurt? If you heard the news, then you know?"

"Then I know what Sam? That you are running out to save a grown woman with a family of her own. She has a husband that loves her just as I love you. You can't be everywhere all the time."

"You know what that, was an awful thing to say. You can be really harsh at times. I love you Charles. I will see you soon. Thank you, for picking up the kids." Sam hung up the phone. She turned on her blue tooth and put her earpiece on. She started on her way.

****

Charles reluctantly hung up, and disconnected his phone from his car charger. He was fed-up with the club rules of sisterhood. Trying to shake the thoughts of envy from his brow, he was reminded that a member of his team was not accounted for.

Justin, friend, family, and business partner, had yet to check in with him either. Justin had phoned Charles about a

~ 68 ~

meeting with a client that he needed him to head out in light of his Family trip. He was so caught up with chasing his secretary and hiding his gambling debts he simply forgot. Charles was often preoccupied with Sam and the kids, finding out about his secret obsessions with cards, horses, and sport bets. He could handle his indiscretions it was Sam he couldn't deal with and her meddling sister, Joy.

Charles worried that without Justin, he would become lost in his own mind. Without Justin to calm his nerves, the straight and narrow path he fought hard to emulate, would be lost in the winds. After all, Justin had become the big brother he never wanted; but realized he needed.

~10~

THE INVISIBLE WALL

Joy came from within her shell, and decided to shake herself back into reality. She had drifted into a cocoon of worry and destitution, afraid to come to the realization of the inevitable. Sounds of unfamiliarity came from what was left of her living room. Without a second thought she pulled herself up from her knees and dusted her fears to the wind. Stepping high and fast over the debris she flew from her den and ransacked the gentleman from behind like a 300 pound full back. Wrestling the man down to the ground, her hair clouded her vision. Beating him about the head and shoulders she yelled murderous, threats and obscenities as the man begged for his life.

"Please, I am not an intruder. I'm here to help."

Joy ignored his plight. "Get the hell out of my house, you thief."

"Please lady I can't find my wife. I am looking for her and other survivors." Joy stood up slowly still holding tightly to the man's worn sweatshirt. She wasn't sure that she could trust him. Joy could admit that she did seem a bit deranged. She was screaming and howling like some crazed animal that managed to escape its cage.

"Cut the crap! I seriously doubt your wife would be in my home."

"Oh really," The strange man straightened his stance and wrinkled his brow. He folded his arms across his chest and prepared to be enlightened by her ideas on the matter. "I didn't know that the tornado had designated quadrants in which they threw people. I don't know where she is. I have scoured the entire neighborhood for more than 5 miles from here. Still, there is no sign of her."

"I'm sorry," Joy looked down at her hands that were still trembling with fear and rage. "I don't know what came over me," Joy looked down at her hands as her heart softened. "I didn't mean to hurt you. I just didn't expect anyone to be snooping around in my home. It's amazing how people become so helpful during times of trouble. Instead of trying to help others most are too busy trying to help themselves. What is your name anyway?"

"It's Mike," He smirked scooping out the room. Mike traced his hands along Joy's mantle, and picked up one of the figurines. He tossed it in the air as if to toy with Joy. He knew she was concerned about his presence and beyond agitated. He smiled her way and placed it gently where he found it.

Mike was a mysterious rogue. He continued his investigation looking high and low around the perimeters of Joy's living space. Joy felt uneasy about Mike and his infatuation with her home and personal belongings. She began to conduct a plan of escape in her mind.

Mike became intrigued at a vase that sat unharmed on an end table beside the couch. He recognized the design. His eyes lit up as he knew that the vase collection was very rare, and over a hundred years old. Not paying attention to Joys growing agitation and worry about his true motivations, he picked up the vase to admire its beauty more closely.

"So I guess you are all alone, huh? My wife isn't here I don't see your husband or any rug rats running about." Mike whistled through his teeth and dusted his hands as if preparing to eat a hearty meal.

Joy cleared her throat, "Get the Hell out of my home." Joy pointed her finger praying to God that she could hold her hand and finger still, hiding the tremors of fear overcoming her cognizance.

"Sure lady, I meant no harm. You got yourself a nice piece of art here. Lucky she didn't break. I wasn't looking to steal. I just complimented you on a fine piece of artifact you have here." The surprisingly cocky man looked around the open room and smiled a crooked smile. "I sure as hell wouldn't call this a home." The man said as he looked around the remains of Joy's beautiful 5 bed room home. He stared at Joy for a moment longer and put his hands down to his side. "Hey let me know if you see my wife, will ya, she owes me money?"

Joy was frightened more than ever he surely had a different agenda. Joy clutched her cell tightly in her palm searching discreetly for her power button. With one push ICE would be on alert. The "In Case of an Emergency," application on her phone was a Godsend. This Mike character was obviously no stranger to the family but none of which she had, had dealings with. It was her only hope that Justin hadn't either. The fact that he had her home address is what stifled her with fear.

Mike pointed his finger at Joy immolating a gun and pulled the trigger. "See you soon." Mike scurried out the new exit to Joy's home and was gone with the wind. Joy's entire left side of the living room was completely gone. It was like they were standing in the middle of the twilight zone. Privacy and their rights now exposed to the public.

Joy looked out into the open space, and remembered how close she came to finally feeling safe and comfortable. Her home was destroyed. Her vision blurred and filled with tears, as she walked among the destroyed pieces of her most treasured items. Joy called out to God for help. She was becoming weak with emotion.

Joy's home phone began to ring. Just hearing a sign from the civilized world gave her strength. She was weak with emotion; but filled with the yearning to survive and bring her family home. Joy wiped her face and fled about the rubbish on a search to recover her phone.

"Come on Damn it." Joy was frantically throwing around the fallen pictures, lamps, and cushions. "Ring…Come on, I'm here I just need you to ring again damn it." Joy was so frustrated. It was lost among the rubbish.

She fell down to her knees and began to scream. She began to cry hysterically. "I've got to get out of here. I need to get to my family."

After a few moments alone with her break down she recovered with a new found passion to rescue her children. She looked up suddenly as if she could hear their voices calling out to her. Joy cleared a path, so she could put some things she would need for her trip to the side. "Where the hell is my purse?" Joy quickly thought aloud as her memory was jogged. "I need to phone Darrin."

~11~

GONE WITH THE WIND

"Hello?"

"Yeah, where the hell have you been? I have been trying to reach you for the last hour. What's going on?"

Joy looked down at her receiver to realize that he hadn't been in touch with Ashley either, "Darrin!"

Darrin was still ranting on as he had yet to learn the news about the terrible storm that had hit the Northern parts of California.

"SHUT UP, for God Sakes." Joy began to sob slightly as she quickly recovered to see if she could get some answers to the mystery. "Darrin where is Ashley? Is she ok? Did you get to her in time?"

"What are you talking about? You're kidding me, right? Joy I was calling you to see if you had in fact really put her on the damn train. I haven't heard a thing, and the people here at the train station are saying that they don't even have her train number listed as one of the trains operating today."

Joy sighed at the sign of some hope. "Oh ok," hoping he just got her train numbers confused she ran for her purse to pull out the itinerary for Ashley's trip, "Darrin?"

"Yea I'm here."

"Her train number, what do you have? I have train number 913."

"It's 923," Joy said plainly.

"Well that figures. I guess I heard something else."

"Ok! Darrin hurry up and see what you can find out. I will hold the line. I am so nervous. I am praying that the train is just running late. Please hurry. I have to make sure she is ok so I can try and get a hold of Justin and the boys."

"Wait Joy what's going on? Has something happened are you ok?"

"Yes I'm fine." Joy's break in speech was clearly a sign that she wasn't fine at all. She was quite fragile at the present time, and she still melted when Darrin asked her about her personal comforts.

"There was terrible storm it touched down just a few hours after Ash's train let. Justin and the boys were headed towards Yosemite. My home is in complete shambles. I'm worried I haven't heard anything on the news. There have been reports about all kinds of tragic accidents and fatalities. I still however haven't heard anything about Ashley I just recovered my phone and purse from all the rubbish. I got hit in the head with a shelf down in the basement. I don't even know exactly how long I was out before I came too."

"Joy I am going to find Ashley. Then I am coming to get you. We can find the boys together."

"What about Justin?"

"What about him?"

Joy didn't bother to argue Darrin's immaturity at the present time. She needed to find her family. Her heart and chest was hurting so badly, she could barely catch her breath. Joy paused for more than a minute. The anxiety was becoming far too much for her lungs to bear.

"Joy you there? Are you ok?"

"Yes, Yes. I'm here. Just see what you can find out. I need to make a few more phone calls. I am just a little light headed from the blow."

"Joy maybe you should get to the hospital, and get yourself checked out. I can take over the search from here. I am sure Ashley is fine."

"No! The county hospital has been shut down. It sustained far too much damage to take on any emergency victims from the storm. I would have to travel way across town or to the shelter either way is about an hour drive. I don't have that kind of time. The fatality rate is climbing by the minute. I need to get a hold of Justin and the boys. You handle Ash. I have tried her cell a number of times but it's more than likely out of reach or has lost its signal if it's not damaged."

"Will do, but Joy?"

"Yes."

"Please slow down. You need to stay as calm as possible. Your health is at stake as well."

"Ok I will. Now go find Ash. Please. I will call you again in about an hour."

"K, Bye." Darrin hung up hurriedly and ran to the customer service desk. He grimaced at his parting words to Joy. "K," Darrin remarked as he took his place in line. "That was beyond weak bro, way to hide your true feelings," Darrin lectured himself as he moved slowly through the line. He waited in line impatiently. Darrin pulled the wrinkled paper from his pocket. Shaking vigorously, he unfolded the paper in his sweating palms and read the numbers to the clerk.

"Sir, how may I help you?"

"Yes um, I am looking for this train. Train number…" Darrin paused as he tried to read the blurring numbers off of the small crumbled piece of gum wrapper. He was nervous and scared, and suddenly felt as if he were going to throw up.

"Uh…Yes train number 923. I am looking for my daughter she was coming in from the Martinez Amtrak Station. Is the train late? I understand there was a storm down that way."

The clerk looked off to her right, and appeared to get uncomfortable. Darrin immediately picked up her discomfort and grew agitated. "Ma'am is there something wrong? Where is the train?" Darrin's voice grew louder as he failed to keep his composure. When the clerk didn't respond he grew angry. She placed her hand over her microphone and exchanged a few words with her colleague. Darrin angrily slammed his fist into the Plexiglas-glass window to grab the attention of the attendant.

"What the hell is going on?"

"Sir, Please. We are checking out that train number. The train 923 was involved in an accident we lost all communication with the train about an hour ago. Technicians have gone out to see what they can find out about the train and its passengers. We have yet to receive any information, but if you would take a seat we will let you know of any updates on the matter. I am truly sorry that we cannot be of more assistance at this time."

Darrin began to sob immediately. "Do you have any idea of the severity of the accident?"

"No sir, not at this time."

Darrin's stomach dropped to his feet. He slowly crumbled

the paper in his hand and walked over to the waiting area. His hands were shaking violently. Darrin sunk into one of the metal chairs, as his phones vibration rattled his pocket. Startled by his phones panic ring he shook and scooted to a standing position, almost as if bugs were crawling all over him. Slightly embarrassed he regained his equanimity and answered the phone.

"Damn it Joy," he muttered as he began to speak. He left room for very little response on Joy's end. Darrin was fully aware of how Joy loved control. She would stop at nothing to monopolize the entire conversation. Dictating to him his next move, Darrin was sure to state his case before she could demolish him with her questions and blame.

Even still, years even after their relationships end Darrin felt obligated to rescuing Joy and seeing to her happiness. Darrin rubbed his eyes trying to focus. She was needy but she couldn't blame her after all the hurt and pain she endured during her childhood. He just broke, Darrin knew his love for Joy would never dissipate but he couldn't heal her wounds. He awoke one day to realize that perhaps his devotion to Joy was out of guilt. Though he loved her it would be impossible to mend the fences torn apart if she couldn't first learn to love herself. She would never let him in, not completely. She harvested her fear of abandonment and it ultimately destroyed the both of them.

Darrin swallowed hard and answered the phone call.

Straightening his stance he coached himself to act like a man, "Hey Joy, I haven't received word yet on Ash's train. The attendant asked me to have a seat in the holding area, while they checked the status of the train. All lines of communication were lost when the storm hit so they don't know what the location is on the train. They sent out an emergency car with tech. support. I am nervous." Darrin's voice was beginning to crack as the emotion overwhelmed him. He was finding it very hard to keep from breaking down on the phone with his first love. However he didn't want to alarm Joy, since she was dealing with the missing boys as well.

Joy was quiet. She was stunned at the horror in Darrin's voice. He hadn't done a very good job of holding in his emotions. She realized that he was merely trying to shield her from possible devastation, but she couldn't rest until she knew the exact whereabouts of her family. She could tell that he was keeping something from her. All she could think about was getting off of the phone with him so that she could call the train station herself and get some definite answers about the whereabouts of the train and her daughter. "Ok well just stay put, and let me know the minute you find out something. I am getting ready to head out."

"Head out, where?"

"I am going to drive up the mountain. I want to see if I can spot Justin's car. Maybe go up and help the highway patrol find survivors."

"Joy, I don't think that is the safest thing to do. I think you should stay put and stay near a phone. Let the police and emergency personnel handle this. Have you tried to get in contact with Jakes mom? Perhaps she has heard from him. Is she ok? Was she caught in the storm as well?"

"No." Joy didn't seem too much concerned either way. She couldn't believe that Darrin suggested she sit tight while her husband and children were missing. "No. Justin's mom is out of town her and her sister went back home for their annual family reunion. We weren't able to attend. I had the book tour, and Justin had the camping trip reserved since last year. There was no way he was going to let all that money, go to waste."

"I see. But I still don't think it's a good idea for you to go out on some vigilante rescue mission alone. We need to start an organized search party, with the help of the police. Contact the police and file a missing persons report. Then check with the highway patrol to see if Justin's car has been seen or found."

Joy sighed as her stomach began to fill with worry. She didn't want to accept that something horrible could have happened to her family, but she needed to at least prepare herself for the worst. Somehow contacting the police made things seem too real for her, as if she were sure that they were in trouble.

"Ok. I will contact them right away."

"What about Sam, have you heard from your sister? Is she ok?"

Joy blacked out for a slight second. She was going into panic mode. "No I haven't as soon as I powered my phone back on I called you."

Darrin smiled at the thought that Joy's first instinct was to phone him. He was still very much in love with Joy, but she had moved on and was quite happy. Because of that he too, was happy for her and would never do anything to destroy her happiness. "Call them to let them know what has happened. Maybe they can be of some help."

"Ok." Joy hung up quickly and began to dial Sam's number. As Joy began to dial Sam's number she thought that she should first phone Justin's mom to see had she heard from him. Hanging up on the second ring she tried to get a hold of Justin's mom, Patrice.

Patrice answered the phone on the first ring. "Joy, are you alright? I heard about the storm we are trying to catch the next plane out. Where is Justin? How are the boys?"

Joy's stomach fell to the floor just as her hopes. She was sure that Justin had called and checked in with Patrice. Joy didn't know how to respond to Justin's frantic mom. She would be sure to blame her for sending them away in the first place. Instead of answering Patrice's questions she began to explain her side of the story before Patrice could accuse her of being careless.

"I'm sick. I didn't want Justin and the kids to know. I was going to be undergoing treatment during the next few days to see if this aggressive new medicine could in fact give me a chance, at a somewhat normal life. I wanted to tell Justin. I just didn't want him to worry. I was going to meet him in Yosemite this weekend."

Patrice cut Joy's explanation short. She didn't care to hear Joy's excuses after the fact. She merely wanted to know where her son was located. "Joy do you know where Justin and the kids are, are they ok?

Joy grew agitated as she noticed Patrice's disregard for her acknowledgements. Joy realized that Patrice was concerned for her son, but it was also obvious that she was to blame for the whole business as always. In Patrice's eyes she had caused the storm and therefore was responsible for her son's whereabouts. "No. I haven't heard from Justin." Joy finally answered. "I called you in hopes that he had contacted you."

Patrice covered her mouth in an attempt to stifle her horrific screams, she feared the worst. "I will be there by tonight. In the meantime call the police and keep trying his cell. He was in the hills so maybe he is just outside of the call area."

Joy sighed with a calming sigh of relief. She had forgotten that the signal was extremely bad in the hills. Perhaps he and the children were still alive, but couldn't call out for help.

"I am going to drive out there." Joy blurted out in the midst of her thoughts of Justin and the children cold and hungry. "There is no other way to find them. I know where the cabin is and if they managed to get half way up the hill to Yosemite, he and the boys more than likely have hiked up to take refuge into the cabin."

"Joy, Justin is a strong man, but in the eye of a tornado. It just doesn't seem feasible. Please, call the highway patrol and see if they can get a copter out to scour the area."

"You're right. I just can't sit here and wait around. I am driving myself crazy."

"You are crazy alright," A voice from behind Joy's ear whispers into her ear. Joy fought to shake the thought. "This is all, your fault. She knows it and so do you." The voice continued to taunt Joy and her senses. Joy shook herself back into reality as she tuned in to Justin's mother calling her name for the third time.

"Joy, are you there? What's going on? Call the police. I am sure they are out looking for survivors in the storm. Maybe they have already found some individuals and are waiting for family to contact them."

"Okay, ok. I will."

Joy hung up and noticed the red light blinking on her phone. Scrolling down her missed calls, she noticed Justin's number. Joy nearly dropped the phone from her hands as she hit her voicemail command in hopes for a miracle.

~12~

LOST AND FOUND

Darrin plopped down into a seat in the waiting area, he twiddled his thumbs as he waited for the train station clerk to come and speak with him. Darrin was startled at the phones ring, he was afraid that it was Joy. He was still waiting to find out some information on Ashley and knew how irate and upset she could get. Darrin fought hard to keep Joy in the best of spirits. She had been good not to report him to the child support agency, or hassle him for cash tediously.

"Yeah"

"Hey son, let me speak to my grand baby. I want to make her a special dinner tonight. I am at the grocery and want to get an idea of some of her favorite foods." Darrin's mom was so excited she hadn't noticed Darrin's solemn voice. She had ranted on for an entire minute before checking to see if Darrin was still on the line.

"Honey you there?"

"Yeah Mom," Darrin sighed and breathed in deeply before continuing.

"Mom Ashley's train hasn't come in yet. They say the train was caught in the storm."

"Storm…?"

"Yea, it's bad. I don't know…" Darrin's voice trailed off as he fought back tears. His hands and voice were so shaky his mother could barely understand.

"Now Darrin, listen to me." Darrin's mother Linda was from deep in the south much like Justin's family. The only difference is they seemed to be somewhat California grown where, as Justin's mom sounded as if she had just flown into town the night before. Her accent was just as prominent as if she were fresh from the cotton fields. "Darrin calm down. Has anyone reported on the status of the train?"

"Not yet, I'm afraid. I know Joy is going to blame me. I was always worrying her about sending Ashley down. The second she decides to compromise this shit happens."

"Darrin, Ashley is your child too. You have every right to see her, and participate in her life. You cannot beat yourself up about this. You don't even know if Joy is thinking along these lines."

"No! I know Joy, and honestly if it were me; I'd be thinking the same thing. She is scared and hurt. I am just praying that I can report good news, news that would set both our hearts and minds at ease to some extent. At least if Ash is ok, she can focus on finding Justin and the boys."

"Justin and the boys are missing too, Oh my God. I will start praying."

"Once I find Ash, I am going to fly out to help the search party."

"Well son, that is commendable. Are you sure you will be welcomed? I'm sure his family will question your interest in helping."

"Mom I love her, and if finding Justin will make her happy, then that is what I will do? The children are my main concern. His Family should be able to get past any pettiness in regards to my past involvement with Joy. Family is Family, and now is the time we should all pull together."

Darrin was busy with his speech to his mom that he hadn't noticed the station clerk approaching.

"Hi, Mr. Lang is it?"

"Oh Mom it's the train teller. He is here to give me some information. I will give you a call back as soon as I know something."

"Alright son, just be patient and try to remain calm. I will be praying."

Darrin hung up nervously and addressed the man standing just in front of his path, rather close for his comfort. The attendant adjusted his pants and shook his leg as if to unravel his boxers.

Darrin became instantly aggravated.

"Yes, call me Darrin." Darrin stood to shake the man's hand. He wiped the sweat on the front of his hooded sweatshirt and cleared his throat. "Is everything alright? Were you able to find my daughter?" Darrin starred deep into the man's hazel eyes to see if he could get a reading on the man's demeanor. It was obvious that he too was unsure how to answer Darrin's questions. He appeared to be slightly nervous and shaken as well.

"Sir If you would come with me?"

Darrin nervously nodded and gave a hand gesture to lead the way. Darrin dug his hands deep into his worn jeans, as he took the walk down the long corridor which seemed to grow thin as walls passed. The walk was quiet and long. At the end of what seemed to be about an hour walk they were greeted by a suit just in front of a large door.

"Hello Mr. Lang. I am sorry to meet under these circumstances; but I would like to ask you a couple of questions."

Darrin's heart sunk almost immediately as his knees buckled from beneath him. Darrin breathed in deep trying to regain his self-possession. "Yes of course anything you need."

"Well I understand you were inquiring about your little girl. Was she traveling on a train today?"

"Yes."

"I see. Sir was that train number 923."

"Yes it was. I had to call her mother to verify the train number. I was so nervous about seeing Ashley, I wrote the train number down wrong. I'm sorry, Um Mr….."

"It's Detective."

"Detective…."

"Just Detective"

"Ok… Is everything alright? Have you found my daughter?"

The Detective shifted his feet as he adjusted his tie. "Mr. Lang if you would take a seat?"

"I'd rather stand." Darrin clinched his jaw and planted his feet firmly onto the floor, in an effort to prepare for the news.

"Please Mr. Lang, you should really sit down."

Darrin reluctantly took a seat and folded his hands onto the metal table. The fear on his brow peered back at him as he starred at his distorted reflection in the mirrored metal surface.

"I am sorry to tell you this but; train 923 was taken by the storm. Our rescue crew went out to the tracks where the train lost communication. The train was completely taken apart by the winds of the tornado. Our men are making every effort to comb the area for survivors we have recovered several bodies from the wreckage. We have two young girls among those that were recovered. We would like to see if you could identify either one of these victims as your daughter."

Darrin began to cry violently as he pulled his wallet from his back pocket. The detective instructed the attendant to take the photo and match it up against the photo in the file. The attendant didn't speak but made a confirmative head gesture to the Detective.

"Sir is she your daughter." The Detective laid an opened manila folder in front of Darrin with a Polaroid picture of a girl, with the words Jane Doe written on the bottom. Darrin afraid to look at the photo raised his eyes slowly to view the body of the little girl. He knew as soon as he saw her hands. She was wearing her birthstone ring he had purchased for her on her last birthday. Darrin began to scream as he fell to the floor of the interrogation room. He sobbed pulling his legs close to his chest he made a tight ball to comfort himself. He wept like a child. The Detective excused himself from the room.

"Take as much time as you need. I am sorry for your lose."

"How am I supposed to tell her mother that her little girl is gone?" Darrin stood to his feet with his hands out stretched towards the heavens. He was visibly shaking and looked as if he were going to pass out at any given moment.

"Sir...Sir... Mr. Lang. I think you should sit down." The attendant noticed Darrin shifting from right to left. He was unsteady and mentally unstable. "Mr. Lang I am going to call an ambulance and get you some water. You don't look so good."

"I'm fine." Darrin fell back into the metal chair nearly toppling to the floor.

"I will be right back with that water. Stay put!" No sooner had the attendant sped from the room, Darrin wasn't two steps behind him venturing into the opposite direction. Darrin had to get to Joy and tell her the news before she heard it in a broadcast on television. They were sure to be releasing the photos of recovered passengers on the train soon. He needed to get on the first thing smoking towards Northern Cali.

Darrin blew past the waiting room with blurred vision. He caught a distorted glimpse of a little girl standing with a worn doll and a torn journal with the words, "Ash," printed in jewels on the front.

Darrin's chest tightened as if his heart were being squeezed. He smiled slightly and slowed his pace as he began his walk towards the journal. Darrin was nervous and his hands began to perspire. In such a tragic event the last thing he wanted to do was approach this small child only to find that she wasn't the finder of his daughter's journal and traumatize her more.

"Excuse me I don't mean to bother you." Darrin rubbed his hands like a shy kid.

The little girl's mom recognized the resemblance of the girl that saved her little girls life. "Your daughter saved me and my daughter's life. She was very brave. My daughter kept her journal in hopes to give it to her; but…" The little girl's mother hung her head. She couldn't bring herself to utter the words.

Darrin nodded with agreement and smiled a shaky smile. It took everything in him not to break down and cry. His heart was broken and to see a little girl survive the incident he was both envious and elated that his daughter traded her life for another. She died a hero.

"Here Mister…," The little girl stepped forward and took Mr. Lang's hand. I couldn't find Ashley but I found her journal. I hope she is ok." The little girl handed Darrin the rugged journal and bowed her head.

Darrin smiled as he took the journal from the girl's hand. "Thank you so much. I am sure she is ok." Darrin bowed to thank the girl's mother and shook the little ladies hand. He strutted away without a second glance afraid the tears would give away his sadness.

~13~

THE RAT RACE

Darrin took a cab to the Los Angeles Airport. He was too shaken to drive. He paid a parking fee to leave his car at the train station and left with just the clothes on his back. Good thing he was now the owner of the security firm he was once for. His job was the only thing that kept him out of trouble. The street life was a hard thing to ditch, and frankly all he knew how to do was hustle.

The traffic to LAX was gruesome as usual. The nervousness settled into Darrin's stomach when, they finally got about three blocks from the drop off. Eager to get to Joys side he decided that to wait for the traffic to let up, would be wasting entirely too much time. Instead he paid the cab driver, and jumped out.

Darrin ran through traffic sprinting like a track-star, high-knees and all. He got half way up to the ticket booth when his phone rang once again.

"Yeah," an out of breath Darrin answered.

"Darrin is everything ok?"

It was Sam, calling to see had Ashley made it to Los Angeles. She was in traffic herself.

"I'm on my way to Joy. I can't get her on the line. I am so worried. Did you pick up Ash? Have you talked with Joy this evening?"

"No!" Darrin's speech broke. He didn't want to alarm Sam or tell her that Ashley was a victim of the storm. He hadn't even talked with Joy yet. However, he was finding it hard to keep it together, as if the reality of the situation was just hitting him.

"I am on my way to her now. I want to help." Darrin hung up to avoid any further questioning. Sam was good at interrogating individuals, and he couldn't stand her either. She was such a, "Bug a Boo." His entire relationship with Joy involved Sam and her needs as well. Sam was full of it, and always doing something she had no business. It didn't help that they shared the same face. Genes were a questionable fact. Darrin couldn't understand how someone with the same genetic make-up could be so different.

Darrin ignored the vibration of his phone for the second time. He was sure it was Sam wondering why he hung up so abruptly. He had no answers for her. She would soon know, but not before Joy if he could help it.

Darrin managed to snag a seat on the next flight that was leaving less than 15 minutes. He was excited about being able to get to Joy in such a short time, but his chest hurt in that he was going to be the bearer of bad news.

Stumbling onto the plane, as he nearly tripped over his own shaky feet, he quickly sat and flagged for an attendant. Darrin whipped out his identification and asked for the strongest thing available along with an icy cold beer.

"Sir is that all?"

"No, I'd like some of those complimentary honey coated peanuts, and a miracle if you don't mind."

The attendant chuckled. "That bad huh…? I think I can manage the peanuts. The miracle is another story. However, I have heard a number of beautiful stories about the beauty of flying and prayer. Something about being closer to God that makes things a little better."

"Thanks, I think I will try my hands at that. It's been awhile since me and The Ole Guy spoke."

Darrin closed his eyes for a few minutes to see if he could focus on putting the pieces of the last hour together. He couldn't begin to think of a way to tell Joy about Ashley. The drinks weren't much help either. The reality was heart wrenching. The numbness he was looking for, to at least calm his feeling of guilt and helplessness, had abandoned him.

****

Sam slammed her fists into her steering wheel. She was so frustrated about the traffic situation she thought about just turning around. She hated when Charles was right about something. He would never let her live it down. She wanted so much to rescue Joy. She could care less about the argument her and Charles would be sure to have upon her return.

"The kids are fine." Sam noted to herself. "Charles can handle picking them up, and getting them fed."

Sam's thoughts quickly shifted back to Joy and the kids. She smiled slightly, finally the hero. Sam wondered why Darrin was in such a hurry to get to Joy himself. Was he trying to win back her love, after all these years? He hadn't dropped his careless, loose living ways, since Ash was born. Guilt can be a silent killer. Perhaps it was time for him to show face.

Sam reset her phone to see if she could get a signal. She hadn't talked with Charles since she left. A simple one hour drive had turned into three. She was sure he was worried. The phone rang several times and still she got no answer. She hung up and phoned again. Perhaps he was driving? He should be wearing his blue tooth at any rate. Sam didn't truly trust Charles as far as she could throw him. There were a number of indiscretions in their marriage that surfaced. It seemed like every year there was a misc. chick coming out the wood work, to let Sam know of Charles and his extra-curricular activities.

Sam wasn't at all innocent. At least two of their children were in question. She was easily persuaded to seek counsel in other men, when Charles was out and about. Sam was in a vulnerable state often and men tend to take advantage of women in these states. She used that fact to her advantage as well. She wasn't always the victim. She learned how to use those same men to get what she needed financially. Most were married themselves, and couldn't risk losing their families over a one night stand.

Sam cleared her head. As much as she wanted to make it to Joy before the rest of her family she knew that, that would be against all odds. Traffic was heavy. Ciaos was a mist, and her tank was a little on the empty side.

"Damn it!" Sam cursed when her red light came on, if that wasn't a sign? Charles had yet to return her phone calls. Sam and her car troubles would add fuel to the fire already enraging Charles. Sam thought if she could just make it to the next exit, she would be able to get off the highway and pull into a rest stop. Otherwise she was sure to be a victim to quite a few drivers and their smoldering road rage.

****

Charles' phone was ringing off the hook. He looked at the caller Id and flipped it over. The kids were safe and sound and in their room, so there was nothing to discuss with Sam. His biggest worry was Justin, and the gang that he could have sworn was following him on his drive to pick the kids up from school. Charles was fuming with anger to think that Mike had administered goons to follow him, around as if he weren't good for the money. Charles had to admit that his gambling had gotten beyond out of hand. He was borderline bankrupt. Justin was not only his back bone but his financier. He knew he could call Justin and he would bail him out. Although Justin didn't know why Charles needed the funds Justin would up the money, because of the kids.

The last portion of loaned money was truly to pay the loan sharks before they broke both his legs and torched his 2011 Land Rover. Justin paid the money because he thought that Sam was spending frivolously, and because of her carelessness the mortgage suffered. Without Justin, Charles was sure to feel the blunt of his misappropriation of funds.

His gambling problems and free for all dating would bury him alive, He had to find Justin. He was his life saver.

Besides, that he was happy to say that his meeting with a lucrative granting agency went extremely well. He was excited to report the good news. Charles took a sigh of relief that he was at least listed as one of the beneficiary's to Justin's estate, he frowned upon his jealousy however, because he actually had something to leave to his wife and children. If Charles passed in a freak accident that very moment he would leave nothing but a bunch of debts that his wife would surely have to tend to, or be next on the hit list.

Charles' phone rang once more. He slammed the remote to the television down and huffed as he answered with a frustrated greeting.

"What's up?"

"Charles it me Sam"

"Yeah I got that, from the caller id. What's up? Is everything ok?" Charles was not at all interested in Sam's whereabouts or the issues of her day. His voice was dry, and lacked emotion or remorse.

Sam began to cry immediately. She was so fragile. The traffic was frustrating, but more so than that she was upset about the fact that Darrin would get to Joy first and therefore become her hero for the day. It pained her greatly that she couldn't win for losing in every effort she made to one up Joy, or at least prove to her that she needed help as well.

"I get it, you are angry with me, but you have to understand that I needed to go and make sure Joy was ok. She is all alone."

"I get it, and please Sam. Spare me the drama of you wanting to help. You forget I know you well. You want to play captain save a hoe, go right ahead. I mean that in the best way possible. We both know I am the one that married the hoe." Charles was nasty in his remarks and looked for the go ahead to continue in his spitefulness. He was irritated himself, worried about the possibility of being followed. His kids were heavy on his mind. He dare not blink too long for fear someone would enter his home unannounced.

"You know Sam? We just may have issues in our own home we need to tend to. It would be nice if I could count on my wife for a change. I realize Joy is your sister. I also realize that she is about the only person you can count on when you are in need of help. But I think you tend to forget that, you can't be of any assistance to others if you can't help yourself. I need to go. I want to get the kid's bath going before the movie comes on. I don't presume you will be joining us for our family night will you?"

"Charles."

"Never mind, I am sure you have better things to do."

Sam just hung up the phone, as she thought about the truths of Charles' argument. "It is AJ's world, always has been. We are just living in it." Sam cursed as she remembered Joys break down of her prize possessions. AJ's world was simple. It was the initials to her name, Justin her husband and her 3 children all beginning with either the letter A or J. She proclaimed that all her actions were to secure the needs and safety of her family. That was why she worked so hard, went back to school, started her own business, etc., etc. Sam shook her head and put her blinker on to signal her desire to get into the exit lane of the freeway. Sam was going home to her family. They needed her far more than Joy did. She would call her later to make sure she that was ok.

~14~

WAKE UP!

Joy floated up to her bedroom to change into some warm clothes. Her new air conditioning system worked far too well, the mirrors and pictures that hung throughout the first floor of her home were cold and foggy. As she neared her bedroom door her stomach began to quiver. The thought of having to sleep in their bed alone was frightening. Joy ventured into her walk in closet, her favorite part of the home. She carefully slid her hands along Justin's side of the closet caressing his garments. She smelled them to see if his scent still lingered within them.

As she drifted off she began to pull the shirts and jackets from their hangers and put them on, she warmed as she wrapped the overgrown sleeves around her small frame, and smiled at the thought of him holding her in his arms. Joy thought about her counsel with Dr. Zimmerman, as a voice from behind threatened her wavering sanity.

"You know you should have kept up with the counseling. I know I could use a tall cold drink and maybe a Demerol, let's not forget that cute little orange pill of yours Fluvoxamine."

Joy began to shake rather violently, as she shut her eyes tightly. "Go away. Please. Now is not the time."

"Awe..., poor baby. I didn't know you had scheduled times for your psychotic breaks. How is the medicine treating you? You know the ten thousand dollar treatment you traded your family for? What was that drug called? Oxycodone was it?"

"No! It was Voriconazole. What can I do for you?"

"Oh nothing I just came to see how ghastly you have managed to louse things up this time."

Joys head began to hurt so bad she heard sirens and the room went completely dark. She could no longer see shadows or flashes of objects that helped her identify her way around. Scared that the bump of her head had caused actual neurological damage she scrambled from beneath Justin's clothing, to locate her migraine medication."

"Looking for these?" The splitting image of Joy stepped into the light and tossed a bottle of pills onto the floor just in front of her. "You should really take those things regularly. I hate how people misuse medication. They never follow the regime and wonder why the symptoms worsen, or the drug stops working all together. Pick up the pills and take one, or two. Why are you doing this to yourself, Mrs. Anderson?"

Joy crawled towards where she heard the pills fall onto the rug, reaching helplessly she grabbed for the pills, only to grab a handful of shaggy carpet. Joy's face hit the floor hard as she was exhausted and out of breath. She had only moved inches, but the adrenaline she used to keep panic away from the pain she endured exhausted her.

Joy's mind went blank as she drifted into a coma of uncomfortable memories. She found herself on the couch of her most dreaded place. At Dr. Zimmerman's office along with his prying beady eyes and his psychological speeches.

★★★★

"I heard about your thesis. I thought your synopsis on stress, had entirely too much medical jargon. I mean you did want those of different backgrounds to get the just of your argument. I paid close attention to your theories of the mind and stress. I found it hard to put together. How can one thought be hypothetical and a proven theory at the same time?"

"Well my friend that is because it wasn't a theory. It was a hypothetical question I posed in order for individuals to ponder their responses to the situation. As you have and proposed that it didn't make sense."

"It was preposterous, inhumane."

"Inhumane? How can you categorize a human emotion as one that is inhumane? It may not be socially acceptable but it is certainly not inhuman. It is quite popular might I add, no matter how frowned upon the notion."

"I see."

"What…, are you immune to the realities of the world?"

"No. Just don't feel as if this is my area of expertise, nor my problem. I was hoping to discuss my personal issues. Not your thesis on the mind. I merely mentioned that I had some recollection of the piece, which I found to be distasteful."

"Well while I am sure you have a well-developed analysis in regards to my work. I too, have a report to expose."

"You know that I wish I could tell you something that would be exciting to talk about amongst your colleagues, but I can't. My spiritual inhabitant doesn't appear with some mystical cloud of smoke, or theme song. She is ruthless. She takes control of my mind and leads me to believe that I am in control. She ignores my thoughts."

"I find that quite hard to believe. I believe you are in complete control of this so called personality. She is a part of you, you know. She simply acts out all those suppressed emotions you try so hard to hide. She doesn't hold back those emotions, because she doesn't have that type of control. You should be prepared to answer to those she comes in contact with. Maybe just maybe she is your way of exposing those truths that may be keeping you locked in a box. She needs you just as much as you need her. Regardless to how out of the ordinary this may seem to you. The two of you must come to some sort of understanding and compromise. How do you think we as humans normally work out the good and the bad? Do you honestly think that all of us are not faced with this issue? I fight the torment each day, simply stress's that may just push me over the edge. It may be time for me to sit in your seat and tell all. I am plagued with thoughts of hurting those who have hurt me. I too, think that I am entitled to fairness and at times wouldn't mind taking the law into my own hands to cool my britches."

Joy's nose flared. She was enraged at the Doctors analysis of her multiple personality. She all of sudden grew hot and sweaty. "If you don't mind, I need a drink of water." Joy excused herself to visit the ladies room. She bolted down the long hall she could hardly stand enclosing walls of the psychiatric office and Dr. Zimmerman's beady eyes judging her. Joy locked the doors of the bathroom and let out a loud sigh of relief. She rushed to the bathroom sink and turned on the faucet. Joy rinsed her face vigorously, as she peered into the vanity mirror.

"Keep it together Joy. Can't you do anything right? You are shaking like a leaf."

"The shaking is just a simple side effect of the medicine. I don't feel a thing." Joy stood speaking into the mirrors reflection motioning her hands to add clarity to her argument. "I'm just lingering around. I hear nothing. The children look like they are laughing and playing but I don't know why. I have no desire to entertain. I am just here. Wishing I weren't, or at least wishing I had some reason to be here. Like my presence is needed. These pills make me feel sober, solemn, and slow. I don't have the spunk of my usual personality, when I am around my husband. I don't stress about the children and their wellbeing, eating, shelter. Things that matter, don't you think it's important for me to at least care? I understand my issue with stress. But at least I cared. I worried. I had empathy for those wronged or harmed. Is this really your idea of healing, my mind is in more disarray than it was before. I feel like my brain is scrambled."

"I'm tired, sleepy." Joy's reflection replied, dismissing her entire speech on the matter. "I don't think I want to talk about this right now. You are under a lot of medication and you yourself have no idea what you are talking about. Why don't we revisit this some other time, Shall we? I mean really. You seriously think that you have no need for meds? You are talking to me for God sakes. Isn't that enough of a reason? I asked you to get help. Doctors ordered you to sleep. He ordered you to change your diet. You decided to take a pill, the quick fix. I think that the meds will work, if you stop abusing them.

"Abusing them, you are the one who showed me how. I guess that was when the actions of drugs benefited your desires. Now that I can't think straight, you abandon me. Just like everyone else. I don't have the steady hand to do your dirty work any longer. You are just like everyone else. How could even you abandon me.?"

"How can I abandon you Joy? I am you."

Joy slammed her fists into the mirror. The pain of the blow shook her into reality as she realized she had been gone for quite some time.

****

A shaken Joy awoke, and looked around at her surroundings. She seemed shocked that she was in her closet back at home. Joy tried to regain her composure but her thoughts ran continuously wild. She sat upright into a pile of Justin's clothes in their walk in closet.

She was going crazy thinking about all of the things that could have happened to her children and husband. Joy began to rock slowly and whisper words of comfort, when there was a knock on her front door. In addition to the heavy knocking, they rang the doorbell in an alarming frenzy.

Joy staggered to a standing position, as she danced and jiggled her way out of Justin's over-sized clothing. She quickly grabbed for a sweat shirt and headed towards the front door.

Jogging down the stairs she grabbed for her flashlight just in case she were about to be confronted by another so called drifter looking for survivors of the storm.

"Hold on! I'm coming."

Joy unbolted the front door as if the left side of her living room was still intact. She opened the door slowly to preview her guest. It was the police. Joy's stomach dropped and a huge lump formed in her throat. She was having troubles breathing as she slowly opened the door. The police officer had a small leather bound note pad and when he realized he was about to address a woman he immediately removed his hat.

"Mrs. Anderson?"

"Yes? What can I do for you?"

Joy could barely breathe. She placed her hand over her chest and placed her other hand on the sill of the door to hold herself up.

"Ma'am may I come in? I would like to talk to you about Mr. Anderson, Is He your husband? We traced the license plate numbers of some of the vehicles that were found in the storm and this address came up in our system. Do you happen to own a 2011 GMC Suburban?"

"Yes. Is everything ok? You found my husband and children?" Joy was ecstatic. "Well are they ok?" Joy buckled through the door and shoved past the decorated officer to peer out at the cop car in hopes to see her missing family members wrapped in blankets. Nothing was there. Joy solemnly pulled herself back into the inside of her doors frame and starred into the eyes of the officer.

"I am so sorry." The officer began. He was having a bit of trouble explaining his visit, as if he were a rookie. The officer cleared his throat and began. "Your car was found halfway down the cliffs of the mountain. Most of the cars found had been thrown off of the road and into the forest. They were killed instantly by the impact of the winds. You will be happy to know that your husband and two children didn't feel a thing."

Joy looked at the officer more puzzled than ever. She was clearly lost and had transposed into something demonic in a matter of mere seconds.

"What the hell do you mean, pleased to hear, Is that the best you can do? Oh your husband and children were killed in a tragic tornado. They were blown off a damn cliff pummeling to their death, but not to worry they felt nothing. Did you recover any bodies? Will I be able to identify them, to make sure, I mean…?" Joy was deranged and slipping out of control. She was yelling at the top of her lungs. Residents that were still in their homes stepped out onto their porches in wonder of the matter.

Joy turned her attention to her nosing neighbors and stepped out onto her porch to give the spectators an accurate view of the show. "Hey everyone, this nice gentleman, compliments of Oakland police department has come to inform me that my children and husband were killed in the storm; but I should thank my lucky stars that they didn't feel anything. Well, guess what? I feel it. I feel the pain. I feel the wrath of the storm. Why didn't it take me too? What point are you trying to prove, God?"

The officer looked nervous and pulled his walkie from his side pocket to call for back up. He was in no way prepared to deal with the emotional tirade Joy and her multiple personalities had unleashed.

Joy turned around and stumbled back into the home. The yelling and screaming exhausted her and she suddenly felt the urge to lie down. "If you don't mind Mr., whoever you are?" Joy backed slightly from the front of the door and blacked out almost instantly.

Falling back as she nearly fainted. Darrin caught her mid-air. During the ruckus she hadn't noticed his cab pulling in. He went around to the side of the home and invited himself in. It wasn't hard the entire wall was missing.

Joy both stunned and amazed, spun around without hesitation to greet who she thought to be Justin.

"Justin is that you? Oh my God I was so worried."

"Sir, may I ask you who are, and how you are related to Mrs. Anderson?" The officer budded in to make sure that Mrs.

Anderson's guest was a welcomed one.

Darrin stood still, unable to move or respond, he couldn't understand Joy's state of mind since he was standing in plain view. Darrin had no idea of Joy's disability. She could see flashes of black and white rarely in color. The migraines made her sight that much worse.

"Joy it's me Darrin." Darrin finally managed to speak when he noticed Joy was staring straight through him. He ignored the police officer's line of questioning and continued to console Joy, "Are you ok?" Darrin figured she had just gone into complete shock.

Joy was stumbling into a breaking point close to the edge and fast. The entire room began to darken. "Darrin…" Joy's lips began to quiver as she used her hands to search for a place to sit down. She was sure she would faint. There could only be one reason why he would come to see her.

"Here, let me help you."

"Ma'am do you know this man?"

Joy threw her hands up immediately. "No, I can do it myself. What on earth are you doing here? I thought you were going to call me? What's happened? Where is Ashley?"

"Yes officer, he is my daughter's father. He was supposed to be picking up our daughter from the train station this evening; but we lost communication during the storm."

~ 113 ~

Darrin was silent and sure he was dreaming as he couldn't believe he was standing in the same room as Joy. His mind was racing and he couldn't pull himself to reality.

The officer lowered his eyes at Darrin and excused himself from the couple. "Ma'am, here is my card. We will be in touch. Any items we can salvage will be returned to you when the construction and clean-up begins. Here is a bag of the belongings we recovered from the car. There is no need for us to keep them since this is obviously ruled out as a death by natural disaster. I will leave you two to catch up." With that the officer departed and jogged to his patrol car. Joy stood with her back turned to the door as she didn't bother to acknowledge the officer and his gesture of sentiment. She was in shock to see Darrin standing in her living room. He didn't have to say a word, his presence said it all.

Joy fell into Darrin's arms. She cried violently. Enraged with fury she pummeled her fists into Darrin's chiseled chest. Darrin didn't say a word all He could muster was his grip. He held onto the small of Joy's back as he caressed her hair.

Darrin closed his eyes wishing he could take the pain away. He cursed his thoughts. They were traveling at high speeds, towards his overwhelming passion to reclaim his first love. Joy's mind raced. Her heart sunk and for a moment she lingered on towards a quick escape from the hurt and pain that was sure to suffocate her. Joy lifted her head. Her brow met his full lips.

Darrin kissed her softly on her forehead.

Joy fully aware of her growing vulnerability feared she could not be responsible for her actions. Her alter ego lingered near and her overactive libido was sure to indulge in such pleasantries.

Joy's sudden urge to rekindle the spark was unsettling. Quickly, she gathered her senses and tore herself away from Darrin's advances. Joy apologetically tapped her hands upon Darrin's chest, and walked over to the brown paper bag. Darrin was disappointed but, adjusted the bulge of his pants as he stood to help Joy.

Joy could smell him approaching. She focused on the bag. The room was black. Sitting in the center of blackness was a grayish white bag. Joy could see nothing else. She feared what was inside. She prayed for the strength to search its contents. Darrin made a few steps towards Joy. She was standing so still as if she had been confronted by a ghost.

"Joy..."

"I'm fine. I just...I," Suddenly Joy recalled her conversation with the police officer. "He never said whether their bodies were recovered did he?"

Darrin placed his hand gently on Joy's shoulder praying he didn't startle her. He was so confused. He didn't know what to say, for fear he would upset her further. "No, he didn't," Darrin calmly spoke.

"No he didn't, did he?"

~15~

THE TRUTH HURTS

Patrice landed at the San Francisco airport just two hours of speaking with Joy. She was anxious to get to Justin and the children. Joy had yet to phone on the status of the search, so she was unnerved. Flagging down a cab she threw her overnight bag into the front seat and asked the driver to take the quickest route to Oakland. The cab driver looked concerned and asked if she knew about the big storm that had hit the city. Patrice, a bit agitated ignored the cab drivers small chatter. She advised him to pay attention to the road, especially in light of the storm and the high traffic of police and pedestrians.

Patrice tried Justin's phone once more, she had phoned him over 20 times since her plane touched ground. She was horrible at sending text messages so she didn't attempt. However, it was unlike Justin to ignore and neglect to return her phone calls. Patrice's chest grew tight as she listened for the phones ring and a familiar voice to greet her on the other end. Instead the answering machine chimed in. Patrice smiled at the sound of Justin's voice. It was the only thing that seemed to keep her hopes afloat.

Patrice laid her head back onto the cab drivers shabby leather seat and drifted off. She was exhausted from the flight, and experiencing jetlag. Swerving in and out of lanes the cab driver sped through the back roads of the city to avoid the traffic and blocked areas of the storms greatest destruction. Shaken by the turbulence of the cab's stunt driving, Patrice was shaken out of her sleep to catch her cell phone ringing for the second time.

Patrice fumbled through her black snakeskin satchel in search for her phone. The phone silenced. Patrice was so emotional her desperation to get to her son drew tears to her eyes. She finally managed to find her phone, and looked at her missed call list. Her heart sunk when she saw Justin's name and number appear as the last call she had missed just moments ago. Patrice began to scream with cheer startling the cab driver to nearly hit the car just in front of him.

"Oops I'm sorry, Chile I didn't mean to scare you." Patrice apologized with a huge smile. Her nausea subsided within that very moment, as she realized her son was ok. Coming down from her celebration she decided that she had better return his call, as he too could be worried about her and her whereabouts. Patrice hit her call back button and awaited to greet her son with a warm welcoming, "Hello and Thank God You are ok."

Patrice sat anxiously on the phone as it rang for the third time. When she didn't get an answer she started to worry again. Just as she were about to hang up and call again she heard an answer on the other line.

"Hello."

Patrice nearly dropped her cell phone in her lap alarmed and taken back at the voice on the other line. It was not the voice of her son Justin. It was Joy. Patrice couldn't even imagine why she would have his phone at such an hour. Her only excuse to even answer his business line was if Justin had specifically instructed her to, if he were expecting an important phone call and needed a message taken.

"Yes, Joy. It's Patrice. Where is Justin? I see you have his cell phone, so he and the kids must be alright?" Patrice sat waiting on Joy's response on pens and needles hoping that her assumptions were correct.

"Uh, Mom, I think you should come home as soon as possible. The police just left our home about twenty minutes ago. Darrin flew in. There gone, Patrice. There all gone."

Joy broke down in tears as she hung up the phone. She couldn't bear to hear Patrice scream for her son. Nor could she take the mental and emotional beating she would be sure to give her. It was obvious that Patrice blamed her for Justin and the children leaving town in the first place. Joy just couldn't take dealing with the bad mouthing and scrutiny of her decision making process.

Patrice was stunned to hear the news of her son and grandchildren. She held the phone to her ears and zoned completely out. Patrice's eyes were as still and clear as glass, and her body was as if made of stone. Her skin paled, and her knuckles turned white.

"Ma'am you okay?" The cab driver inquired as he pulled up, to the front of Joys home. "From the looks of it you, can't even tell that there was a tornado, from the frontal view of the home." The cab driver chuckled, trying to make light of the situation. He noticed an entire wall was missing from the side of her home. "You don't think any of your family members are still here do you? You sure this is the right address? Surely they have gone to the shelter. It's just not safe around here after something like this happens. The freaks come out at night. There is looting, and violent crimes are high on the rise. I don't want to leave you here if your family has gone to a nearby shelter. I will take you there free of charge if you like?"

Patrice stared at the Anderson home now in shambles. It was a work of art. A home both Joy and Justin designed and paid for together. Now after a storm the foundation was a mess, but nothing their insurance couldn't handle. Joy would surely have to move into something a little more conventional until the home was repaired. Patrice handed the cab driver a fifty dollar bill and grabbed her bag from the back seat.

"I'll be fine. Thank you for the offer." Patrice closed the door of the cab and stood on the walkway before taking her walk to the inevitable. She didn't know what to say to Joy. She had just lost all three of her small children, and like her she'd lost her son but he had already lived. She couldn't imagine having to deal with burying her babies. Still, Patrice straightened her stance and walked confidently up the walkway and onto the porch to ring the doorbell. Thinking about who Joy said was in the home with her she thought she'd better just walk right in. She trusted Joy, but she didn't trust this mystery man. Patrice always identified Ashley's biological father as the mystery man, because he was in and out. He never stayed long, if he showed face at all. It was in fact a mystery why Darrin would be down in their parts in the first place.

Patrice used her spare key to the home and casually unlocked the front door. The spare key was Justin's idea, just in case of emergencies. According to Patrice it was for her to check things out from time to time to make sure everything was copasetic.

Patrice threw her satchel and overnight bag onto the bar stool in the kitchen and looked around for something to drink. She almost never drank unless on special occasions, but she felt as if she needed something to ease her anxieties. Scouring the kitchen cabinets and small wine pantry she found a half empty bottle of wine. Patrice pinched her lips tightly together as she peered around the corner of the kitchen which led to the hall leading to the den and second floor.

The damage to the home was pretty extensive. There was a gaping hole in the living room wall. The housing and construction department did a pretty good job of putting up some type of tent contraption to separate the outdoors from shelter, but it wasn't at all livable in Patrice's eyes.

Patrice grabbed her satchel and headed towards the den to take a look around before venturing upstairs to the guest bedroom. It was her favorite part of the home, since Justin designated the peach room for her visits. It was also a master suite. Patrice loved the peace and quiet of the night and the fact that she could easily get to and from the bathroom without hassle during the night. She was getting old and the trips to the potty were far more frequent than she'd like to admit.

Patrice peered into the den to find Darrin sprawled out on the sectional. He was wrapped in one of the good downing comforters Patrice picked out and had the nerve to be lying under a blazing fire. Patrice could have ripped the blanket from off him and tore him from limb to limb, but she was tired herself. She simply went upstairs to check on Joy and go on to bed.

MY NEMESIS, THE MIND'S EYE

Aija M.Butler

~16~

BLIND FOOL

Joy tossed and turned as her counseling sessions with Dr. Zimmerman haunted her emotional stability. Joy could feel the cold air hitting her bones as if she were naked. She sunk further beneath her bedspread and grabbed hold to Justin's full size pillow. She couldn't sleep. Flashes of Justin and the children danced in her head. The memories were clouded by visions of their faces that she could see so clear before her accident.

****

"Joy wake up," Dr. Zimmerman clapped his hands in an effort to awaken Joy from her hypnotized state. He was exhausting every avenue known to man to get her to open up and discuss the issues regarding Joy and her abusive childhood. It was evident in prior meetings that Joy harvested anger and resentment.

Joy sat up on the couch and grabbed her head. It was pounding again. "What happened how long was I out?"

Dr. Zimmerman blinked at Joy, but didn't respond verbally.

"How is your eyesight? Have you had any visual hallucinations, what about voices?"

"I can see clear as day, while on medication. I can't explain how she can see and I can't."

"I see… I took a look at your file." The Doctor looked over the brim of his glasses and focused on Joy's face.

Joy was agitated at his lack of response to what she thought was a major issue. "Well then, we have no reason to talk today do we?"

"Not if you don't want to, but I think we should."

"Well I will pass if you don't mind? Don't worry I will be sure to cut you a check for the hour of power. I'm beat and I would like to go home and get some sleep."

"That's wonderful. However, you and I both know that you don't sleep. So why don't you and I just cut the Bullshit." Dr. Zimmerman crossed his legs and folded his hands.

"WOW, such language doc? Now you're talking. I better sit down. Do you have one of those long rulers too?"

Dr. Zimmerman smiled at Joy's new quirky attitude. It became immediately evident that the woman he was speaking to was not Joy. Her demeanor was raw and sexy. Dr. Zimmerman's client stared him down and blew a kiss his way. She sat close to the edge of her seat and opened her legs wide and undid the top button of her blouse, fanning her chest as if it were hot in the well ventilated room. Dr. Zimmerman noted her change in persona and gave the woman his undivided attention.

"So, why don't we start with your name? It's clear I am not speaking with Joy any longer."

"It's Lillian, Lillian Andrews but you can call me Lilly for short. I am named after our mother."

"Lillian…," Dr. Zimmerman's eyes lit up.

"Yes, Lillian. I am the third child left to rot in our Mother's womb. Joy has become a great success. She is a bit on the weak side but she is very smart. Sam on the other hand is a mess. It's embarrassing that we share the same traits, physical traits." Lillian looked up at Dr. Zimmerman to make sure he made note of their conversation. She wanted to be sure that he knew the differences between Joy and herself.

Dr. Zimmerman looked puzzled as he flipped through Mrs. Anderson's chart. There wasn't a third baby listed on any of the medical charts.

"Don't bother," Lillian interrupted the doctor's concentration. "You won't find anything. I was absorbed into Joy's tissues during the second trimester. So I guess you could say that Joy is essentially two different people."

Dr. Zimmerman's mouth was wide open with surprise. He was intrigued by such a case. He could almost see his name printed on the cover of the next issue of the American Psychology Journal.

"I am a demon child." Lilly fluttered her fingers as if she were a monster. She enjoyed toying with the doc.

Dr. Zimmerman adjusted his glasses and wiped his brow.

Lilly closed her eyes briefly and paused as if Joy was resending into her rightful place. She then opened her eyes suddenly and wide, as she began to laugh at the doctor's facial expression. "This is going to be so much fun." Lillian smiled generously and took off her heels. "I have been waiting for a long time to come out and play. There was no way I was going to continue to let you or anyone else intimidate fragile Joy any longer. She has done her time. I think it's time some people get a taste of their own medicine. Fight their damn battles if you know what I mean? From now on, I'd like you to deal with me entirely. Those pills you gave Joy are doing her well. She sleeps. That is something she rarely does."

"Who are you?" The doctor never looked up from his pen and pad as he began to write anxiously, his thoughts.

"I am named after Leliel Andras, angel of night, ruler of deception and quarrel, death to be exact. I am the true angel of Death," Lilly stood embracing her glory and expanded her arms as if allowing her wings to spread. Dr. Zimmerman's eyes bucked with a sarcastic gesture and wrote vigorously.

"Really...?" Dr. Zimmerman excitably interjected. He bit his lip in shamefully as he hurried about adjusting his seat and clearing his throat, desperately trying to regain his composure.

"Uh, no…, sounded good though didn't it? I am Joy, her true personality, one in which she has fought so hard to keep a secret from others. However I think it's time that Joy sit back and let me handle things. Don't you think? I mean she has been run straight into the ground. She has her own husband and family to deal with. She can't keep tending to others and their individual trials and tribulations. It is one thing to be there for others; but it's simply unfair to carry the entire load. My back hurts from all the piggy back rides, Joy has been issuing. This accident with her eyes, made room for me. After the car accident, her mind was open to new things, people and areas of her brain that she had yet to use. Don't get me wrong Joy is brilliant. She just isn't a fighter, no matter how hard she wants or tries to get others to believe. It's always been me." Lilly looked onto the Doctors face.

"If I didn't know any better, it sounds as if you are suggesting that Joy is expendable? Would you care to enlighten me? Mind manipulation is one thing, but entire body inhabitance…" Dr. Zimmerman closed his eyes. He was both confused and growing angry.

Dr. Zimmerman began to feel as if Joy was merely playing games to avoid talking about the issues regarding her family. Inventing this no nonsense character was just a defense mechanism, a poor way of dealing with the matters of her troubled heart and mind. "How are you going to get Joy to surrender her soul? She would never leave her family."

"She will if she has no reason to stay. Joy is going to be so miserable. She is going to feel her skin tearing. Her life dissipating as the foundation of her home crumbled around her. She will be disheveled filled with uncertainty and disdain. I will be there to comfort her. I will tell her that it was her family that facilitated her demise. I came to ask for help, hoping to gain restitution for my evil deeds. I worked for her betterment, not to destroy her.

She will say that things are fine, but we both know that they aren't. They haven't been for quite some time. It's time for Joy to grow some balls. Stand up to people, stop being the red carpet under others feet. Her heart will be black as coal, eyes cold as ice. Much like the persons she has helped over the years." Lillian smiled as she sat back to ponder her plan briefly. Even she was concerned about Joy's ability to withstand and overcome her advances.

"So you think Joy would be better off if you were the dominating personality?"

Lilly's lips curled frightfully thin, as she was angered by the Doctors probing questions. "I have no intention of hurting Joy I'm here to help her. She needs me." Lilly tried her best to sound soft and sincere.

Joy's doctor simply stared at Lilly from over the brim of

his bifocals. "If this isn't the biggest load of bull I have ever heard? Do you seriously think that you could just waltz into a professional Psychiatrists office, feed me a few lines of bullshit to see if you can manipulate me to do what you want? Well I'm sorry, Lillian. I am Mrs. Joy Anderson's Doctor. If you are need of counseling services, I am afraid you are going to have to schedule an appointment, or find yourself a Doctor."

"Well isn't that sweet. Creative even, but I think the two of us know that it's not going to be that easy."

The doc just stared for a while and decided to play along. "So how can I help, can I offer you a cup of coffee, some water perhaps? Your hour is just about up."

"Cute how very cute, Joy is here, she just can't come to the phone right now, if you know what I mean?

Dr. Zimmerman cleared his throat and interjected Lilly and Joy's thoughts. He sat upright in his chair and scooted to the edge of his seat. It was no doubt in his mind that during her brief silence Joy was communicating and desperately trying to force her way out. Lilly closed her eyes and let out a frustrated cuss. Dr. Zimmerman noticed Lilly's discomfort. He began to speak low, saying the same things over and over again. It was if he were chanting to conjure up spirits. Lilly turned away from the Dr.'s wrath to gather herself. Joy was returning and Lillian couldn't stop her. Dr. Zimmerman used words and conversation topics that he and Joy shared to gain the attention of Joy.

When questioned about certain subjects, Joy usually spoke as if her confidence had been ripped to shreds. Her heart began to beat rapidly and her knuckles turned white. She was gripping the edges of the leather couch, in hopes of regaining control of her mind and body.

Joy tried to focus, but she was still quite confused. Her eyes opened as they were shut tight. They were now hazel, although moments before they were darkest of browns Dr. Zimmerman had ever seen, almost black. Dr. Zimmerman made a note in his small leather pad and refocused his attention on Joy and her transformation.

"Joy we need to speak." Dr. Zimmerman finally managed to find words. He was in awe of what had just occurred. He sat witness to quite a few things in his time but nothing as sci-fi as this.

"I need to speak with you fast," Dr. Zimmerman, put his hands in the air to signify how important it was to get through to Joy. "Joy, can you hear me? How long can you keep Lillian at bay?"

Joy was shocked when Dr. Zimmerman said Lillian's name. "You saw her? So now you believe me?"

Dr. Zimmerman, put his head down and began to twiddle his fingers. Joy didn't have to ask what Dr. Zimmerman was thinking. The silence spoke for itself. Joys head began to hurt once more. The bright lights were causing her damaged eyes great pain. "Are we done here? I think I need to get to a quiet and dark place. The migraines are beginning to take their toll on me."

****

Joy's pupils moved rapidly under her forcibly closed eyelids as she fell in and out of a drug induced sleep. She had managed to find a few Trazadone pills swimming in an old pill bottle at the bottom of her medicine bag, anything to numb her pain and perhaps rid her of the nightmares.

Patrice peeked in on Joy before she went down the hall to the guest room. She didn't want to disturb Joy. She knew it had been a troubling day for her and she was not in the proper state to discuss the next steps in preparing to say good bye to Justin and the children.

Patrice was surprisingly calm. She lost her parents at a young age and had spent most of her life caring for others. She hid her emotions mostly to protect herself from vulnerability. She would have a good cry in the confines of her room, but never in front of her children. She didn't want to alarm them. Raising Justin alone was a frightful circumstance being that she had him quite young and her husband was killed in the war. She had no childcare and she was still too young to work in many industries of the work force.

Joy was quite lucky to be in a place where both she and Justin were established career wise, and having children wasn't much of a burden except for the actual labor. She smiled at how she'd always teased them about having a few more. She would be glad to move in and play nanny for the first year or so, so that their work wouldn't be affected. Justin Jr. and Josh were thirteen months apart. Rambunctious four and five year olds that by her definition, were grown already. Jr. was out and about playing with kids twice his age and Josh was an electronic geek. He loved gaming, cell phones, and computers.

Dear Ashley, Patrice started to get choked up thinking about how much she had grown. Twelve years of age going on twenty-one. She was a fashion diva, and sports fanatic. How she juggled the two was still a mystery to Pat but she loved the fact that she was a force to be reckoned with.

Patrice's lips began to tremble as she thought about her childhood and the loss of her parents. She was saddened about the loss of her grandchildren. She didn't know how or what to do for Joy, but she would start with a word of Prayer. Patrice quietly closed the door to Joy's room and floated down the hall to the guest room. She needed to get her mind in order. It was sure to be a busy day in the morning. Joy needed to first find a new place to reside, and Darrin's services were no longer needed. If she had too, she would make sure to escort him to the front door.

Settling into her large suite, she tossed back the peach colored iliac spread and jumped into the fluff of the pillows. She was safe in her room, the room that her beloved son designed just for her. She felt closer to Justin than ever. She thought if only she could see him one last time, she would be sure to express how proud and how much she loved him.

~17~

WHISPERS

Joy woke up in a bed full of Justin's clothing. She had tossed and turned all night before drifting to sleep. Finding the pills was a great help. She hadn't heard Patrice come in, but as soon as she woke up she could smell breakfast cooking. For a moment she got excited in hopes that Justin and the kids had miraculously found their way home.

Joy jumped from her bed and sluggishly dragged herself to her master bathroom to take a hot shower. She was in a hurry to wash the stink of the storm off her body. Her arms and legs were badly bruised and the scratches from the wood on her arm stung.

Joy tossed on her robe and slippers and walked out of her bathroom to find Darrin sitting in the middle of her bed.

"Darrin what are you doing in my room?" Joy was startled by her guest, but she felt no discomfort or embarrassment as she slowly closed her robe.

Darrin swallowed hard and wiped the sweat from his hands. "I was just coming in to check on you. Your mother n law is here.

She got here last night. Apparently, she has her own key." Darrin pinched his lips tight, holding back a sarcastic remark. "You know she, woke me up at the crack of dawn with that singing and cooking. I didn't know where I was for a moment. Who could eat at a time like this anyway?"

Joy hunched her shoulders and blew past Darrin.

"Yea, well she isn't cooking for our benefit. She is upset. She either cleans or cooks. I hope you brought your appetite." Joy was nervous, she didn't want to get caught talking to Darrin in her bedroom, while wearing a bathrobe. "Darrin if you would excuse me, I'd like to get dressed."

"Sure." Darrin wore a confused and uncomfortable look on his face. He knew he was being oddly curious and borderline inappropriate but he continued anyway. "What's wrong… you act as if I have never seen you naked?"

"Darrin please you can't be serious right now. Now is most definitely not the right time to discuss our past, a past long over. I just want to get dressed. I don't want to even think about all the things I have to get done today. I need to contact the police to see if they have found my family. Darrin just go please."

Darrin stared at Joy as he began to realize how out of touch to reality she was. "Joy?" Darrin began but Joy quickly put her hand up to ward off his advances. She didn't want to hear him speak of her husband and children. She just wanted him to see himself out.

Darrin shook his head as he turned and walked out of the bedroom door. Joy continued to get dressed. Her mind was wandering and spinning in circles. She became frustrated, looking for a pair of tennis shoes and her sweat shirt to her sweat pants. Joy took all her clothes from her drawers and tore down the garments hanging in her room size walk in closet. Slamming her boxes of shoes to the floor from her shelving she began to scream. She wore nothing but her sweat pants and a floral printed bra.

Joys head was pounding so hard the vision she had left became blurry and filled with spots. Joy fell to the floor in her closet and grabbed for her head. The pain became so extreme she let out another hurling scream.

Patrice heard the sounds from downstairs, alarmed she dropped her glass of orange juice. Darrin ran upstairs to Joy's bedroom to make sure she was ok, Patrice followed.

"Joy you ok?" Patrice yelled up the stairs as she climbed the long winding staircase as fast as her legs could carry her.

Darrin busted the door to Joy's room down tearing the bolted lock from its frame. "Joy you okay?" Darrin scurried around the room in search for Joy. She was laid out in the closet. The pain of her migraines caused her to faint. Darrin quickly scooped Joy from out of the closet and placed her onto her bed. Patrice jolted into the bathroom to retrieve a glass of water, some pain meds, and a cold compress.

Joy was coming to, slightly but she appeared confused. She didn't know who or where she was. Patrice placed the cold compress onto Joy's forehead and asked her if she'd like a drink of water.

"Honey here, sit up and have a sip of this water. I have a few Tylenol to help with the pain."

"No thanks." Joy looked straight ahead, she felt the heat from Patrice's hands on her shoulder and she could smell Darrin's cologne to the left of her but she didn't look either way. "I just want to be left alone if the two of you don't mind."

Joy's attitude was cold and nasty. She felt weird and as if she couldn't control her emotions or her actions. Joy managed to smile slightly to lighten the mood. Darrin didn't buy her sudden change in disposition. Patrice gave Darrin a nudge and asked him to leave the two of them alone. Darrin wasn't at all interested in leaving Joy's side but he left willingly.

Patrice took hold to Joy's hand. It was cold. She folded her brow with worry and looked to comfort her daughter in law. "Joy, I am so sorry. I know that this is especially hard for you loosing small children. I am also in so much pain. I don't know what I am going to do without my son. I want you to know that I am still here for you; we need to decide what we are going to do about the funeral arrangements. I don't want us to have to drag this out for weeks. I was thinking that we could have something as early as next week."

"What! What are you talking about? Joy jumped from her bed and began pacing the perimeter of her huge master bedroom. "What the hell is your problem?" Joy was stumbling around as the room was spinning. She was delirious. My husband and children are out in the woods lost. They are looking for help, and you are here planning their funeral. Damn it!" Joy yelped as she stubbed her toe on her leather ottoman, in the sitting area of her master suite. "Who are we burying, Pat? There were no bodies in the damn car. The police brought a bag full of belongings that were left in his truck. Nothing Justin or the boys were wearing was in the bag."

Patrice stared at a very deranged Joy as the tears streamed down her face. Joy had completely lost her mind as she knew for a fact that at least one of her children's bodies had been identified.

"Joy Honey? Did you look in the bag that was given to you by the police officer that came by last night?"

"His phone was handed to me when the police officer came to tell me the news. Nothing substantial, my husband is alive." Joy's voice trailed off suddenly. She looked in Patrice's direction but it wasn't Patrice she was looking at. She could see a shadow standing just behind Patrice. It was there one minute then abruptly she could hear a small whisper behind her ear. Joy turned her attention to the words she heard whispering softly. She stood like a stoned statue as if she could see a ghost. Again the shadow positioned it's self behind Patrice.

The shadow moved from behind Patrice and stepped in front of her and came close within reach. Joy could see clearly now, that it was Justin. His black and white image came so close it was as if she could feel him standing inside her. She felt her heart jump and warm. Her knees grew weak and the air around the room froze.

"We are ok." The whispers came again as she could feel something brush gently against her cheek.

"Mom did you see that?"

Patrice was still in shock from Joy's outburst. She didn't know how to approach the situation. "Joy I think you should get some rest. We can talk about the funeral arrangements tomorrow. I am going to look into some condos. We cannot have you staying her. Nadine called this morning from the office to send her condolences and she says that she can handle everything at work for the rest of the week. She says she will call you if there is something she needs your assistance with. We are going to have to find a way to get through this, Joy. Justin would want you to. You have a flourishing business with great promise."

Joy sat on her bed. She didn't have anything further to say to Pat. She felt alone. She couldn't understand why no one was interested in finding Justin and the children. They were in such a hurry to write them off as if they were dead.

Joy turned her attention to the brown paper bag that sat on the coffee table in Justin and Joy's sitting area of their room. Her eyes began to well with tears as she wondered what the contents of the bag may be. Could his wedding ring be in the bag, his wallet, something more personable than his cell phone that he could have just left behind in a sudden rush for survival? Surely, they couldn't base his death upon finding his cell phone in the car. That would only help to identify that it was his vehicle.

Joy continued to ignore Patrice's presence. She decided that perhaps maybe, Patrice hadn't gotten the hint that she wanted to be left alone so she laid down and took refuge underneath her covers. Joy could hear Patrice sigh as she collected the wet towel from the side table to take it to the bathroom area.

"Mom could you close the door on your way out, please?"

Patrice, no longer feeling the need to force the situation obliged to Joy's request without a word. Closing the door behind her she decided to put Darrin to work. They were going to need to start packing up the home. Anything that was damaged would have to be thrown out, and anything else worth saving put in storage. Patrice thought it best to start fresh and anew. Joy would do better in a completely new setting. Constantly hovering and burying herself in the confines of Justin's things would send her into an emotional tirade of dysfunction.

A change of scenery helped when she lost her husband to the war. Patrice picked up a phone book and got a realtor on the line. She didn't want to fool around long, she needed to get Joy settled into a new place by night fall. Patrice was uncomfortable herself, staying in a place where loved ones had once lived. It was as if she could hear small whispers in the wind, as she floated about the home.

Whispers of death and anguish, it was horrific the cold breeze that chilled her bones.

~18~

LOST

Sam's alarm went off early morning, but she was too tired to get up and get the kids ready for school. Darrin called with the news of Justin and kids. She wasn't up for much of anything. Charles left late night after the news and had yet to return home. He hadn't answered any of her phone calls, so she was equally worried about him and his whereabouts.

Charles didn't take bad news of any kind very well. News of this caliber could be devastating. Justin was more than a business partner to him. They were like brothers, blood cousins in reality.

Sam forced her way out of bed. She could hear her tribe wrestling in their room. The arguing and bickering had already begun. It was time for a referee to step in.

Sam jumped from bed and marched down the hall to her son's room. Her three boys were in action, bickering over whose turn it was on the video game. Sam stepped just in front of the television to get their attention.

"You boy's get this room cleaned up. It's my turn," and with that she snatched the controllers from each of the boys and turned the television off.

"Not a word, until this room is spotless."

Sam left the room and made sure that the door was open so that she could hear if any ruckus were started. She sprinted back to her room to get dressed. Today was the day to move Joy into her new condo and she didn't want to be late. Charles was M.I.A., she was sure he would come home to help her out, but he had been so distant it was any wonder where his thoughts were.

****

Charles pulled up to the Anderson home in blur. He had been sitting out in the car for at least an hour when he spotted Darrin coming out the front door. He was hauling some boxes out into the rental truck. Charles lowered his eyes stunned that he had, had the nerve to show up after so many years of absence.

Charles fought to pull himself together. He turned off his cd, and locked up. Bouncing from his car, he strolled up the walk way and caught Darrin's eye.

"So what brings you by the Anderson estate, my cousin ain't even cold yet and here you are pushing up on his girl."

Darrin turned around and flexed the muscles in his jaw

bone, "You here to help or talk. If you here to talk we can set up some other time to do that. I don't get down like that anyway. I am here for moral support. I lost my child too Chuck."

Charles gripped his belt buckle, animating how he felt about Darrin's little speech, "Moral support? We don't need your moral support brother. Joy would have liked a little child support."

Darrin threw his hands up and drew them close to Charles' neck. "I'm warning you Charles. Now is not the time to discuss any quarrels you and Justin may have resting on your scrawny chests. I am here to help Joy. So do what you need too?"

Charles walked closer to Darrin in every effort to egg, Darrin on. He wanted him to make the first move. He was willing and waiting to finish it.

"What's going on out here?" Patrice stepped just outside the front door. She was wondering what was taking Darrin so long, "There is work to be done." Patrice directed her attention to Charles. "Hey Chuck, so glad you could make it. Where is Sam? We can use all the help we can get."

Charles ignored Darrin's quiet snares and greeted his aunt. "Yes Ma'am, show me the way. I'm sure Sam will be here shortly. I came straight from work. I pulled an all nighter. How is Joy holding up?" Charles walked past Darrin purposely knocking him off balance as he walked by. He could see in Darrin's eyes that he wanted to react; but he wouldn't dare in the presence of Justin's mother.

"She is doing as well as to be expected. She hasn't come out of her room all day; but she soon will have to. I plan to have her in her new place by tonight. The contractors will be here in the morn to figure some estimates and get started on rebuilding. I am not sure if she is going to want to sell this place, rent it, or move back in."

Charles' eyes lit up as he walked back inside the Anderson home with Aunt Patty. He was wide awake now. He was going to have to keep his eyes peeled for things that may be of some value. It wasn't going to be too long before Mike and his bandits found out where he had been hiding. It was best not to give Sam the details or accept any of her phone calls. He couldn't risk putting his family in danger over his gambling debts. She couldn't lie about what she didn't know.

****

Joy busied herself in her room packing her things. She awoke from her nap with a sudden burst of energy. She needed to keep busy. The brown paper bag the officer left continued to haunt her. She wanted so badly to see the contents of the bag, but she couldn't bring herself to open it. Instead she listened to the voice mail Justin left on her phone over and over. She tried to decipher his tone of voice. To see if she could detect some sign of distress.

A clue of some sort, instead she heard him saying that he loved her, and that he would see her soon.

Joy packed all of Justin's things in his suitcases. She folded them carefully. His suits were placed in his garment bag, and toiletries in their designated area. She then did the same for her own belongings. Joy saw this as her chance to get rid of some old rags she had been holding on to. She knew it was long overdue. With the new agency and her magazine she barely had time for routine choirs. Justin was busy with the company as well as the business with the home.

Carefully Joy wrapped all of her African masks and figurines. She was anxious to move into her new condo, only to remove herself from the confines of a home that was once so beautiful. She didn't want the reminder of the storm lingering on.

Joy opened the door of her domain and entered the hall. She was shocked to find Charles there working on the paintings that were hung out on the balcony. She didn't speak. Joy simply put the boxes she had packed and labeled onto the floor and went back into her cave to retrieve more.

****

Sam sped into the driveway of Joy's home. She became infuriated when she saw Charles' car already there. She had been

worried sick. Sam slammed on the brakes and turned off the
ignition when she saw both Darrin and Charles prancing shirtless
out to the moving van. Sam fell from her Toyota with one motion.
She left the kids at a colleagues, she had no choice since her
husband had failed to come home the night before. She had spent
the last four hours combing the city, hoping that she wouldn't find
his car abandoned or get a phone call from the police.

Sam high kneed her way up the drive way stepping over the
beds of flower and rock to get to Charles.

"Where in the hell have you been?" Sam ignored the fact
that Darrin was front and center in all his masculine glory. She laid
into Charles without shame.

"Samantha, why don't you run up and check on your sister?
Grab a box or something." Charles was in no mood to argue with
Sam he turned up his nose, snubbing her very presence.

Sam rolled her eyes and stomped inside. He was right.
Right now was not the time or place. The lump in Sam's throat
began to dissipate. Although, the empty feeling in her stomach
lingered on, she was trying to find the words to say to Joy. She had
been in a daze most of the ride to Joy's home. Still there was
nothing she felt she could say that would remotely help Joy
through this tragic occurrence.

Sam felt as if she had lost her own children in many ways.
The pain was far more than she could bear at times. The night was

long she tossed and turned. When she managed to get a few hours of sleep, she awoke soaking wet from night sweats. She wasn't able to shake the images of her niece and nephews.

Sam ran upstairs to Joy's room. She waved a dismissing wave at Patrice. Patrice was busy packing up the kitchen. Sam was sure she was getting rid of whatever items she didn't find fitting to her taste.

To Sam's surprise Joy was busy herself. She was afraid of what she may find behind the doors of Joy's sanctuary. The room was nearly empty. The boxes were well stacked and labeled.

"I guess you didn't need me after all."

"Sam is that you?" Joy spun around and spotted Sam's shadow in the light. She ran to her and hugged her long and hard. She was so happy to see her other half. She was lost and didn't know what to do or how to get through.

"I see you are up. I was afraid I would have to drag you out of bed. How are you feeling this morning?"

"I'm having those God awful headaches again but other than that, I am just anxious to get into this new place. I need to get settled so that I can get out there and help the search party locate Justin and the kids. I know they are out there. I need to find them before it's too late. I have already lost my daughter. I don't want to just give up looking for Justin and my boys." Joy grabbed, squatted, and lifted two boxes at once and hauled ass outside her door where she had stacked the others for pick-up.

Sam was in shock at Joy's analysis of the situation. Her forehead began to bead with sweat as her palms grew wet. She didn't know how to attack the situation so she excused herself quickly to gain some insight on where Joy's thoughts were. "Hey, I am going to go down and grab us a couple of drinks. I know you must be working up a thirst, be right back."

Sam didn't give Joy a chance to respond she needed to leave the room before she put her foot in her mouth. Joy was the psychology major in school, and she counseled youth through her literary group. That was the very point of her developing the "Blog Diaries."

Her agency gave youth a chance and knowhow by way of effective written communication to openly share feelings they found difficult to express. Journaling had proved to be a very good way of self-counsel and reflection. Sam was in no way credentialed to discuss Joy's mental state. She would be sure to monopolize and challenge Sam's knowledge of the mind and how it worked.

Sam went downstairs into the kitchen to visit with Pat she was interested to know what she thought about Joy and how she was holding up. Pat was making sandwiches on the built in grill of Joy's stove. She seemed to be enjoying herself. The table was filled with cut fruit, green salad, lemonade and fresh baked cookies.

"How can I help you Sam? Lunch will be in about 30 minutes. I don't want the boys to think we are trying to starve them. That Charles is nothing but skin and bones, you feeding him?"

Sam rolled her eyes at Patrice's sarcasm. "He's eating." Sam kept her response short. She wasn't interested in conjuring any drama about Charles at the moment. She wanted to get some feedback on Joy. "What's your take on Joy?" Sam pulled up a chair at the bar and sat down to get a closer look at the sandwiches Patrice prepared.

"The girl has lost her mind if you ask me." Pat let out a laugh that scared Sam nearly to the point of falling from her bar stool. She couldn't understand what was so funny about Joy having a mental breakdown. She had responsibilities.

Responsibility's that needed to be handled. Patrice noticed Sam's nose flaring. "Chile, Joy is grieving. What on earth do you expect?"

"Tears, tantrums, depression, but shear dismissal of the loss will do no good. She can't even admit that they are gone."

"Would you?" Patrice slapped the last sandwich onto her serving tray. She cut them in nice triangular portions and added a few parsley leaves for garnish. "Look the best thing for Joy right now is to first get out of this place. Next, love and support. As long as we are there for Joy, she will come out of this. Just you wait and see. I know that you are worried about your sister, but this is all normal in the stages of grief. I went through some of the same things when I lost Paul. He was my best friend and my lover. Much like Justin was to Joy. I will admit to my ranting about the girl's unorthodox views, but the truth of the matter is that we need to give her space, room to breathe, and let her know that we are there for her whenever she wants to talk. I would recommend that once she comes out of this she seek counseling. Other than that, let's just take this one day at a time."

Pat knew full well that Joy was delusional. She couldn't stand Sam. It would be a cold day in hell before she would publically agree to her opinion on things.

"What about the funeral arrangements, the insurance for the home…" Sam was getting worried about Joy's finances. "Not to mention her business."

Pat wrinkled her head at Sam's obvious deep concern about monetary issues. "Well I'm here, and believe it or not she got a place without any problem. The insurance company's contractor will be here in the morning to handle the estimate and get the work done on the home. Nadine phoned this morning and is on her job. Things will be, "A," ok. We will have to just do what we can in reference to the wake or memorial service rather." Pat washed her hands vigorously, as she explained the plan. She hoped that she made it clear that her services were not needed. If it were up to her, she wouldn't have been contacted at all, her loyalty to Joy as always a question in Pat's eyes.

Sam wiped her hands on the lap of her jeans and scooted down from off her bar stool. "I see." Sam didn't at all understand but, she wasn't going to continue wasting time with Patrice as she cooked Joy's food. Sam couldn't really put her finger on why she didn't like the fact that Patrice was in Joy's kitchen cooking, but it bothered her more than she would like to admit.

Sam grabbed a few boxes to take out to the boys. They had managed to find a way around their issues. Outside the two of them were laughing and joking over a cigarette. "Hey, didn't know we had time for cigarette breaks, but I guess." Sam slammed the boxes down onto the grass next to the moving truck. She strolled by the two men as they starred her down. She looked at Charles and rolled her eyes and extended her middle finger to add to her display of disgust. Charles flicked the butt of the cigarette into the dirt and smashed the remaining burn under his feet.

~19~

FACES

Joy unpacked her home quietly and slowly. Her new furniture was already in her new condo before she got there. She thanked Patrice for handling all of the arrangements, but the furniture was in complete disarray. Joy took some time to set up her home to resemble something suitable to her liking. She hung up some art work and cleaned the counters and mirrors of the home.

Joy pulled the boxes around the floor of her condo she labeled the boxes according to what the contents were and which room they should go. Joy found a big box labeled misc. she sat down in the middle of the floor to take a gander at what was inside.

She was looking for the files that contained the deed on the house and other possessions Justin owned. Justin and Joy made a point of outlining their lives to reflect what they had accomplished, what goals were still on the list of to do's, and in the event that they were brutally killed in some jealous rage, who all of their worldly possessions would go to.

Joy pulled out Justin's file, along with a few pictures that were tucked away in between a few of the files. They were pictures of both Justin, and Darrin. Joy looked at the facial characteristics of both men. She smiled at how different they were physically but, the same in that they had both endured such troubling childhoods.

Both men were so very head strong and stubborn. Their priorities however, were worlds apart. While one became a victim of environmental circumstance, the other used his misfortunes to abandon them.

Darrin born and bred in the streets of Los Angeles, fought against the urge to kill, follow, and possess; as he wished for a life of purity and honest work. Often harassed by the demons of the streets he was tested daily. Failing to beat the rap of his destined way of life, he became one of the people he detested. The hustle became his lifestyle. He'd fallen prey to the land of drugs, sex, and money. He traded the love for humanity for the love of the streets. His child suffered from the lack of attention.

However, he provided materials that he could not otherwise afford had he left his unlawful ways. It wasn't until his own brother's addiction that Darrin began to think about his future. The very drugs he sold were those that his flesh and blood drowned in. Darrin found himself in a deep depression. Guilt overwhelmed him. He too, ended up in rehab. Later, after graduating he landed a job in security. The same security firm 5 years later he now owned.

Justin on the other hand born in the South lands was accustomed to gang violence and the like. Though after his brother was tragically killed, He opted out to take care of his mother. His first instinct was to go out and seek revenge upon his brethren; but he quickly changed course when his brother visited his dreams.

Joy was the first to believe the story of Justin's divine intervention. She too, had had some visitors of her own. Joy had a gift that she'd rather suppress. She could see things, despite her sight deficiency. She often had premonitions of happenings, or an awkward feeling when something was about to happen. Joy cursed her gift especially now that her family had gone missing. Her sightings of the future never involved her, just others. She hated to be the bearer of bad news. So she kept quiet and fled without warning others of the frightful terrors to come. She tried to caution others of the sightings, but more often she was crucified for exploiting such nonsense. She gained a few negative reviews from the public eye. Her mental state was questioned, so she quickly denounced her gift and concentrated on her writing and literary group.

Justin had come along in a time of Joy's life that appeared to be the end. She had been hospitalized for just under a year, for a disease that threatened her life. Daily she had to take medication for the disease that seemed to continue on in its rampage. Justin accepted her for who she was. The scars from the illness meant nothing to him. It was as if he didn't see them. She was beautiful, even when she was so thin he could see her skeleton.

Strangely, he loved her when she was at her lowest of times, all the way through her gaining complete conscious awareness and meat upon her frail bones. They encouraged one another and because of that they had become quite successful. Justin became an owner of a big name construction company that designed office buildings, luxury homes, and art museums. He had always wanted to work in construction, but he was a victim of a stabbing in his early 20's. It had left him with some permanent nerve damage to his back and his lungs weren't fully functional.

Justin was her hero he saved her life. She was going to do the same. Joy scooped up her files and placed the other items back where she found them. She covered the box full of files and slid them back into her hall closet. She was warming up to her new condo. It was a spacious three bedroom tri-floor home. The first floor opened up to a large living room and bathroom. From the first floor the stairs led to second floor which was a huge kitchen with stainless steel appliances and cherry wood cabinets, adjacent to a beautiful den. Justin had designed the entire complex. Joy took great pride, in the fact that she was blessed to have a husband with such great talents. He designed the first home they bought together, her office building, as well as his own.

Joy was falling into a deep depression she could feel her bones ache. She didn't want to get out of bed at times. It was hard for her to look at the kid's rooms and their belongings. Patrice and Sam were upset that Joy wanted to decorate the other room for the boys. She used the third room as a home office. She missed Ashley so much. Every time she saw a picture of her, her stomach got sick. Joy shook her way to reality and grabbed for her purse, she was going to go and see the doctor about getting some medication for her issues. She was smart enough to know that she needed to tackle the situation before the voices returned.

 A week had passed in such a blur the days seemed to run together. The messages on Joy's phone were countless as the mail, was saturated with condolence letters from Justin's clients and business partners. The front entrance to Joy's condo was filled with floral arrangements sent by friends and family. She simply ignored them Joy couldn't understand what all the fuss was about. Folk were acting as if someone had died. Joy was in and out of reality. She told herself often that Ashley was away with her father. She took comfort in her safety, because then she could devote her energy into finding Justin and the boy's without causing Ashley great worry.

~20~

SOMEONE TO LISTEN

Joy dragged her feet up the walk way of the Doctors office. She was not at all excited about her visit. Dr. Zimmerman was full of shit in her eyes. He simply refused to hear her desire to be left alone. It was just too much pressure. His continuous bantering on the issues of her past frustrated her and caused feelings of deep discomfort. Things, she would just rather put behind her.

Joy checked in, and took her seat in the waiting room. She hadn't bothered to comb her hair. She just threw it up into her famous sloppy bun and went on with her day, a pair of clean sweats, an oversized t-shirt, and sneakers. Fumbling threw the closet, she found a t-shirt of Justin's he had worn once or twice. She needed something to make her feel close to him. The pictures only made her sick to her stomach. She ached for his touch. She feared that her memories of him would fade as the days grew far that he had gone.

"Ms. Anderson, the Doctor will see you now."

Joy looked up, shaken from her thoughts. "It's Mrs.

Anderson."

"Yes of course. Right this way." The nurse assistant pinched her lips and motioned for Joy to follow her to the back office.

"Joy! Come in. How have you been?" Dr. Zimmerman's enthusiastic smile and tone drifted slowly as he observed Joy's outer appearance.

"Fine I suppose just want to get this meeting over with, I have things to do. I pick up the kids early today."

"Sure, sure have a seat." The nurse assistant paused at the door waiting to catch the Doctor's eye. Dr. Zimmerman was much obliged to notice her and looked downward with his eyes still fixated on her. The nurse responded quickly with a wide-eyed signal, one they used many times before, and made her exit. Joy was crazy as they both agreed.

Joy looked at the Doctor inquisitively and decided to let him know that she was fully aware of the doctor his assistant's side-note. "I know what you are thinking."

"Oh yea, and what is that Mrs. Anderson?"

"Oh…, that I am crazy, that I am confused and completely out of touch with reality…"

"Well, are you? I can't say that you are or you aren't. I think that with the set of circumstances I would be out of my mind, right about now."

"The over the counter sleeping pills aren't working anymore. I was hoping you could prescribe something a little stronger," Joy started in ignoring the Doctor's comments on the matters of her mental state.

"Well I don't know Joy. I am a little leery about prescribing something stronger. I understand that you are having troubles sleeping, however this is normal behavior during your time of mourning and bereavement. With the depression, adding on a medication for sleep can become both addictive and life threatening. I can't in good conscience prescribe you anything else."

"Fine…" Joy stormed out of her doctor's office without a goodbye. She was so desperate for help she didn't know what else to do. The nights were long and painstaking. She was spiraling into a deep depression. Her eyes grew heavy but her mind wouldn't let her rest. It was if she had passed out during the night hours, when she was able to calm down. Her sleep was restless and filled with nightmares.

Joy could feel her husband and children around her. At times she took comfort in the warmth of their presence, and other times she felt as if they were haunting her and blamed her for sending them away. She felt guilty for lying to them about her health issues. She wished she could just turn back the hands of time. Now she was alone. Alone to face her fears and the demons that took over her mind and body. As much as she wanted to save the good natures of her heart, the pain that followed the loss of her family changed her.

Joy bombarded her way into the elevator nearly running over Nurse Betty.

"Hey! Mrs. Anderson? Is that you?"

Joy kept her head down. She wasn't interested in small talk. "Yeah it's me."

"Joy, its Betty, nurse Betty. How are you? Are you feeling alright? You don't look too good."

"I'm not. My Family is missing and no one believes that they are still alive. I am so frustrated by this. My Family has been busy doing nothing but planning a funeral for bodies that haven't been found. My daughter's body was the only body recovered after the storm. She died in a train accident when the tornado hit."

"Oh my God, I am so sorry to hear that. Joy if you don't mind, I'd like you to take a walk with me down to my office. I am the nurse practitioner here now. I'd like to hear a little bit more about your symptoms. Its sounds like you may be suffering from Dissociative Identity and perhaps even Multiple Personality Disorder.

I know this may sound strange but after you left the hospital after your accident, I took on a study about the mind, how it is altered after neurological incidence and eye sight. You would be amazed at all the findings. How the senses become heightened in other areas. How the brain begins to work much differently as it did before." Nurse Betty was fascinated by her case studies. Joy was equally enthused and confused. She knew that if she played her cards right she could score some drugs to help her get through her long nights. She also knew a great deal about the mind as well. After all she was a psychology major. Joy squinted, her eyes as the blinking light of the hall irritated her spotty vision.

Nurse Betty noticed and quickly made a mental note of Joy's symptoms. "Have you been suffering from migraines long?"

"Almost 10 years now. They started my Freshman year in college, and progressed since then. I didn't start taking anything for them until shortly after my accident. I started seeing Dr. Zimmerman and he prescribed Propranolol, it worked for a spell, but it didn't stop the migraines or the pain."

"They weren't supposed to. They were supposed to slow the progression and incidence of the occurrences. They aren't for pain. They are beta-blockers." Nurse Betty opened the door to her office and ushered Joy to a seat. "Where is the pain located predominately when you have these headaches, and have you noticed a certain time when they occur? Is there some type of trigger associated with these headaches?"

Joy took a seat as she sipped the tea, Nurse Betty set before her. Her taste buds nudged when she smelled the tangy sweet of lemon and honey.

"I'm not really sure if there is a trigger, except stress, and light. I only figure it to be light because there is a sensitive area in my right eye that tends to pain me when a bright image of light hits it in a certain way."

Nurse Betty dropped her pen and pad onto her desk. She was shocked and dismayed that someone issued Joy an actual license to drive. "Joy you do realize that you are legally blind. How and why on earth would you be driving? I am surprised you would even get behind the wheel of a car after such a horrific accident."

"Don't remind me. Who else was going to drive me around? I have a life, job, family to take care of." Joy took another sip of her tea. She was growing agitated with Nurse Betty. Her counseling session was drawing them no closer to what her true desires were, which was to get her hands on some medication. "I can see perfectly fine Nurse Betty. My blindness has changed considerably since the accident. I believe the migraines attribute to my sudden spells in blindness and incoherence. I have been able to see quite well for the last 6 months."

"Really...?"

"Yes Really! For the most part my blindness is in color. At times I cannot decipher the color of things, and at others when the migraines come I grow completely blind. Everything goes black. I can see shadows, as my sight restores."

"What else has been going on?"

Joy relaxed a bit. She sat her cup of tea on the table and began. "I have auditory hallucinations. I can hear them laughing at me. They are taunting me. When I can manage to block out the sounds and screams the visions begin. I try to run and hide in a well lit room, hoping the demons will stay at bay. The movies have it all wrong." Joy laughed a bit slapping her knee.

"What do you mean?" Nurse Betty wondered.

"Portrayal of the super natural is highly unrealistic. I guess everyone is different. I was a fool to think light and a clove of garlic and a cross around my neck would suffice that is for sure. The yelling screams were so horrific my eardrums began to burn. The only thing I could do was try to relax my mind and listen to what and whomever they had to say."

Nurse Betty wrote in her journal her eyes were squinted as she concentrated on the words she was trying to note. "I was wondering if you would mind coming to see me for a while. I am not as credentialed as Dr. Zimmerman but I think I can be of some assistance to you. I want to go over my notes and see if I can prescribe a few medications. I feel that will help us to target the origin of these migraine headaches as well as isolate the incidence when the hallucinations occur.

Call this a hunch but I am not sure that you necessarily

have a mental disorder. The side effects of certain medications that you have been previously prescribed may be the cause. I want you to discontinue the use of any current medication you are presently taking for the next couple of days. You may experience some issues with night sweats, as you will be go through a period of slight withdrawal. I am going to give you something to take the edge off today. However, I would like to see in in a couple of days. I need to monitor you. I want to access your mental state before I issue you the medication I have in mind for you. Does this sound like something you can commit to doing?"

Joy sat upright in her seat. She was a bit worried about having to go through withdrawals. "I suppose. The night sweats couldn't be any worse than what I am already suffering through. I will give it a try, if we can find a cure to these hallucinations that would be a blessing."

"I would also like to get you set up with some grief counseling, for your daughter that is." Nurse Betty meant for her entire Family, but if she was going to treat Joy she needed to first gain her trust. She knew that Joy suffered from some sort of delusional separation from reality. She just didn't know how serious it was.

"Sounds good," Joy had no intention of attending. She casually grabbed for her purse as she accepted the prescription from Nurse Betty. "Thank you." Joy smiled a shaky smile at the nurse. It had been a long time since she was able to do that.

"For what…?" Nurse Betty reached out her hand to Joy. "I am only doing my job. I am glad I ran into you today. You have been on my mind ever since I started the study. I hope that my findings will help you."

"Me too," Joy escorted her way out of the hospital and out to her car. She was anxious to get home. She didn't do so well in public these days. The air felt different. The sun was out but the days still seemed strange and unwelcoming. She took refuge in her three-bedroom home, a safe haven from the world's wrath.

Joy drove home cautiously running every red light she came across. She couldn't understand her own urgency. Joy had been taking pills from every source she could find. She was no longer able to get emergency medication from the mental health department in the county building; but she had gained some use out of her trips to the emergency rooms around the North Bay area. Although she was not welcome to the facilities near her house she had been fortunate enough to get a few pills from the Walnut Creek and Concord locations.

However, grateful for the pills, the medication made her nervous and fidgety. The side effects alone were reason enough to discontinue its use. Joy was much more concerned with her sleepless nights than her days full of solidarity. Her writing suffered, and her business was beginning to feel the blunt of her clouded judgment.

Joy thought about her plans for the rest of the evening as she quickly pulled into the parking area of her new three-bedroom condo. Joy kept the door to the room of her missing children's bedroom closed. She didn't want anyone to ruin the surprise for them when they were found.

Joy was convinced that her children were still missing in the storm and that it was a matter of time before they was found. Anything that she could salvage from the storm she kept but all other things that had perished from the storms wrath she had to let go.

Family photos were damaged beyond repair. The water and mud had soiled them and disfigured the images of her family. She cried softly as she wiped away the water which smeared the faces of her loved ones. Patrice and Sam had to take over the job of packing and throwing things out. She did manage to salvage a number of family photos, photos that pained her to look at.

~21~

A MATTER OF LIFE AND DEATH

Joy walked around her quiet apartment searching for answers. She didn't understand her recent bout with illness. She seemed forever plagued with the fear of death and dying. It had been almost three years since her cancer entered its dormant, but she'd lived each day fearing that symptoms of her illness would resurrect, up until they did. Her chest hurt often, and breathing was a chore.

Since the storm Joy frequently visited the emergency room. She was paranoid and banned from the hospital in close proximity to her home. She was saddened by all the pictures of her missing family so she busied herself removing them from their frames. She didn't want them to see her suffering. Most days she spent her time wallowing in self-pity. Work was the farthest thing from her mind. The house work suffered as well. Since the tragic storm, Joy had lost nearly thirty pounds. She was dangerously floating near skin and bones. Her sister thought she may have been starving herself to death. Sam was always looking for weakness in Joy something she was perhaps better at.

Sam felt as if things came too easy for Joy, that she had to work a little bit harder to get attention or become successful. Joy was also the big sister everyone depended on. She could do no wrong. She always came running when others were in trouble going well beyond the call of duty. She could be difficult to read.

Motherly, of course but, the true aspects of Joys personality was her desire to be loved and accepted. She wasn't interested in respect at least it wasn't at the top of her list. She yearned for recognition. Although as of late, the horrible disease plaguing her caused her emotions to spin out of control.

Joy fell to her knees just beside the bed and began to pray. She was so lost she didn't know where else to turn. God was now her only friend. He was the one and only person she could rely on. She could vent without ridicule and repent for her sins. She worried constantly about others judging her. Even though in her heart she knew that only God could judge her, she still feared the eyes of the world.

Joy stood at bay when important decisions were to be made. She didn't want to be perceived as the heavy. Her business suffered slightly because of it. Good thing, those things that needed a stern hand were written and electronically submitted. She wasn't good with face to face confrontation. Still, she was vociferous and had a way with words, in the developmental stages of profitable ventures.

Slightly shy, she commented on political views only when summoned. She never raised her hand to take charge of things that she herself didn't breed. She worked alone. It was as if pulling teeth if she were forced to ask for help. She would just rather suffer from sleepless nights and poor hygiene in order to get the job done personally. She was afraid that her ideas would be stolen. She couldn't bear to fall into the shadow of another knowing full well the ideas were her own.

Protecting her reputation was just as important as her family. She would fly off the handle and into a murderous rage when her judgments were questioned. Joy's prayers always consisted of one of two things, clarity and wonder.

Joy quickly ended her prayer session when she heard a knock on her door. She was slightly aggravated, but was curious to know who could be interested in her life as a mole. She was literally suffocating to death and had no desire for rescue.

Sam was yelling at the top of her lungs, just in front of Joy's town home. Joy scurried to her feet and made her way to the living room. Tossing on her robe, she grabbed for her pen and pad and threw it over to the couch. She had to set the scene. Joy opened the door slowly and with little excitement.

"Oh Heeeeyy…!" Joy dragged her voice sarcastically and threw on her fake smile. "It's so nice of you to drop by and so out of your way, what's going on?"

"Nothing much can I come in?"

"Sure, why not, would you leave if I told you No?"

Sam pushed her way in with a slight bump into Joy's hip and began to investigate her apartment. "So, how are you doing?" Sam threw her coat and purse onto the chair just next to one of the end tables, and picked up Joys writing pad. "Are you working on anything special?"

"Um not really I guess I have been going through a slight spell of writers block, but I'm sure it will pass."

The meds aren't making you sick are they?"

"I'm not on medication."

"Wait! Excuse me." Sam closed her eyes with disbelief. I'm not following. That medication is to cure your disease. The doctor said that you HAVE to take this medication, possibly for the rest of your life. How could you not be taking it? Have you lost your mind?" Sam stood with her hands on her hips with both irritation and disgust. "After what this treatment cost you. Forget the shame of going to your ex for the money; but the literal loss of your Family."

"Sam, I understand your concern, but please watch it. You have no right mentioning my Family in this. You know why I sent them on the trip. Don't you dare try to insinuate that this whole ordeal is my fault, I didn't' want them to go; but what was I supposed to do?"

"So does this mean you give up? I get it okay?" Sam put her hand over her heart to show both her sincerity and fear. "You are depressed, and you may have thoughts of just giving up, but suicide is not the answer."

"Suicide…" Joy began to laugh so hard she surprised herself.

"Sam I'm not suicidal. I just don't want to be numb. You and I both know those pills do nothing for the disease. It can come back, whenever it pleases. I am not going to wait around for its return. I am going to live."

"You have got to be kidding me. Is this really what you call living? You haven't stepped foot out of this house for weeks. I am surprised you still have a job. Where is the book you were supposed to finish? All I see are papers tossed about your office, blank pages at that, some with one or two words, others with a bunch of incoherent gibberish."

"Thanks Sam, for all of your concern. I really appreciate your coming by, but if you will excuse me I would like to get back to doing absolutely nothing, in peace. I have money to survive on. My company is doing just fine without me. Nadine is a total life saver." Joy was nonchalant and showed little emotion as her voice dragged on. She didn't bother to even look up from her empty notepad. She peeked out from under her bath robe, which now swarmed her. She was thinning tragically. The bones in her face were prominent. She just didn't look well.

Sam ignored Joy's request, and continued on to the next order of business. "The Wake is tomorrow have you changed your mind about attending?"

Joy looked up from her solidarity and rolled her eyes with disgust. She was becoming irritated with her sister's presence and her refusal to leave peacefully.

"No I haven't I will not be a participant in a lie."

"Joy!"

"Sam…"

"Joy, listen I know that this is very hard to accept but you have got to come to terms with the death of your children and husband. I loved them too, Joy but the search was called off over a week ago. We need to honor their memory."

"There is no honor in forgetting that they may still be out there waiting to be rescued. I will not simply give up because others are tired and need an excuse to explain the disappearance of my family. My husband called me, Sam. I picked up the phone and he was there breathing faintly, hoping that I could trace his call. I'm pretty sure someone dead couldn't manage to call me on the phone."

"I understand what you are going through, Joy."

"No the hell you don't! I do believe your children and

husband are alive and well, correct. I never should have sent them away. If I had only been honest about my illness I would have been able to save the lives of my family. We would all be here safe and sound."

"Joy you need to mourn the loss of your family. Hanging on to these hopes is not healthy at all. I mean look at this place. People would think that you have literally lost your mind."

"What are you talking about Sam?"

"Joy the damn table is set for a family of five. You look like you have been up since the crack of dawn making breakfast, eggs, pancakes, bacon, sausage, fruit, who is all this for?"

"My family…" Joy looked at Sam with such terror in her eyes.

Sam shifted her feet and took a few paces back from Joy. "You know what Joy?" Sam said as she lifted her hands in an attempt to surrender. "I think we need to slow down and have a talk. Come on sis. I just want to help. I think it's time you went to see somebody about this."

"I don't need to speak to anyone. I am a damn psychologist."

"Just because you can counsel others, doesn't mean that you know how to treat yourself. You are an emotional wreck. It's best you try and get your life in order. How can you feasibly carry on in your professional career if you are suffering from such turmoil? There is no way you can hide the issues of your life from your work. Your mind is clouded. You are out of touch with reality, and you refuse to talk about what's really going on with you Joy."

Sam pushed Joy towards the master bedroom to see about tidying her up.

Joy broke from Sam's grasp and yelped as if she were being attacked by some unknown stranger. "I'm not going anywhere with you, Sam. You have the nerves, the gall, the audacity to stand there with your bare face hanging out and try to analyze me and my issue. You think losing my family in a freak accident is a fucking walk on the beach. You think waking up every morning only to realize that your family isn't nestled safely in their beds is easy. Just wake-up Joy. Move on Joy, say good-bye Joy. Fuck you, Sam.

Oh and wait, the family, his side of the family as well mind you. Have no problem at all just calling off the search and throwing flowers on a grave. Tell me, Sam how in the hell did they just get you to roll over and accept the fact that your niece and nephews were just blown with the wind. Tell me, how Charles his blood cousin, just in case you all forgot we married into the same family, could just overlook that fact that they had recovered some pieces of our luggage and our car, but there were no bodies in the damn thing now were there? What did the oceans tide sweep their bodies away, away Sam, off of a crowded expressway in the middle of a traffic jam?

Sam, Justin called me." Joy looked almost demonic. She was beyond irate. "He called me, I need to find him. I'm not crazy. I am just frustrated that you people are so quick to just give up on your loved ones. Just carve their names in a cemented plaque," Joy looked down at the floor as the room began to spin. She had been getting severe migraines for the last week almost daily. The pain was horrific. At times she could barely see, and her right side of her face just shut down. She couldn't wait to return to see Nurse Betty.

"Joy, are you alright? Sam noticed that Joy didn't look so good. The color in her face turned almost grayish blue. She was shaking slightly and stopped dead in the middle of her sentence as if frozen in time.

"Joy!" Sam called out to her sister a second time to see if she could conjure her out of her trance. Joy looked up at Sam but she wasn't looking at her. She was looking directly through her. Sam was frightened by Joy's behavior. Joy this isn't funny are you alright? Joy moved her index finger slightly as if it hurt for her to move a muscle. She couldn't speak as she tried to utter the words, "Help!" Again Sam asked if she was okay.

Joy was pointing at the bag on her counter. Sam finally got the picture and grabbed for the bag. As she poured out its contents she couldn't decide what she needed from her med bag that would help her with her current state of paralysis. "Joy I don't know what medication to give you. I am going to call 911. I think you need to get to the hospital. We can always explain to them why you were unable to attend the wake. I want some answers Joy. I want to know how long you have been having these migraines. You may not be able to move, but I know you can speak. You must not forget that I was the one with you when you suffered your first bout with this disease."

Joy gritted her teeth loudly. "It will pass Sam. I have been getting headaches all week. It's just the stress. I am a little worked up is all? The fact that you and Justin's mom keep pressing the issue about this memorial service isn't helping either. I can't take it. I would just appreciate it if you all would just leave me be. You want to say goodbye then go right ahead. I will say goodbye when they have actually gone." Joy winced with pain as she struggled to finish her sentence.

"We are done here Sam. Don't worry about me. If I stand still for a few more moments the pain will let up. I have been suffering from back and neck spasm. They occur whenever a migraine hits. I'm already undergoing treatment to resolve this issue."

"Joy I'm not leaving you like this. You are standing in the middle of your living room like a statue for God sakes. You need help."

"Yeah you are. I don't want to talk to you about this any longer. You are the reason I am stressed now. So if you leave I will be fine. Please go! I can't take any more stress right now. You go and play your part. I don't have time for games. I am going to find my family."

"Your family is dead Joy! Their dead, and there is not a damn thing you can do about it. You can't bring them back. Joy, if you ever want to see my children again you will get help for yourself. I can't have you around with your hallucinations and narcissistic views about the family, my family. So get over yourself Joy you are not the only one who has suffered a loss. We all loved your children and Justin. How do you think Justin's mom feels? She too has lost a child. Just think about it for a minute will you, stop being so damn selfish."

"Yeah Sam, I am sure you have an abundance of love for my husband. You tend to float in forbidden directions, but selfish? You think I'm being selfish?" Joy couldn't believe her ears. She put her hand up against her chest as if she were short of breath.

"How dare you, say shit to me about being selfish? There is no way in hell you can call me selfish, after I gave up my entire life for all of you."

Joy forced her leg to move an inch towards Sam's shadow. Sam flinched warding against Joy's advance. She feared Joy's paralyzed state had passed. She would surely tear her from limb to limb.

"Selfish…, you really should be going now? Thanks for your time and rude comments. If I had the strength I would walk over there and slap the taste from your mouth. You are one piece of work. Let's see just how well you do when dear ole hubby finds out that you have been dishonest almost your whole damn life. Wait until he finds out about your indiscretions. You know what? If I weren't so damn sure that you weren't completely heartless. I would detect just a little bit of satisfaction coming from your end. Could you be happy that I have lost everything? Maybe now you won't have to continuously live in my shadow."

"Joy that's enough, I can understand that you are upset and going through something, but I won't be disrespected."

Joy laughed at Sam's articulation with words. "You know where the door is. Its high time you use it." Joy could hardly contain herself after Sam's choice of words. "HA!" Joy busted out with an over exaggerated laugh of disdain. "I won't be disrespected either. With my most recent issue honey, you would do good to see your way out of here. Sister or not I may start in on you and forget who you are. Don't mistake your blood to make me any difference at this point. Your face and its likeness to my own couldn't save you, because right now I hate myself. I am asking you to leave Samantha there won't be a second warning."

"Alright I will leave you be. Today! I think I may have to pay that doctor of yours a visit. This makes absolutely no sense. If I have to find another care provider for you then so be it. I am not just going to sit by and watch you rot away in this hell whole. You think you could find the time to clean up, during your busy schedule? Since you have all this money, you don't even need to lift a finger. Hire someone."

"Thanks but no thanks I don't need help with the daily tasks of my home. My children will be home from school soon, and I will have the home spotless and their afternoon snack waiting for them. So if you don't mind I'd like to get back to work, and another thing, don't you dare talk to me as though I am your homecare client. I run the affairs of my home and business."

Sam simply stared at her sister with disbelief. She looked down at the floor, before turning on her heel and leaving the apartment. She didn't say a word. Slamming the door behind her Sam looked out onto the road before making her way to her car. "Not for long Sis, not for long."

~END OF VOLUME I~

mynemesisbkseries@gmail.com

http://mynemesisthebkseries.blogspot.com

www.twitter.com/nemesisbkseries

Check out the My Nemesis Book Series on Facebook

~THE SAGA CONTINUES~

With Vengeance Is Mine
VOLUME II

PROLOGUE

"Dear God, Why Has Thou forsaken me? Why must I stay to die…alone in the hellish ways of this world? What am I to do with this life, now that all I have loved and cherished has perished?"

The mind's eye began with Joy's loss of sensibility after her family is taken by the storm. Joy may appear crazy but she will not be taken advantage of, not if Lillian Andrew's has anything to say about it.

As Volume II begins Joy fights to decipher between her lust for revenge and the good natures she longs to promote as she clings to her need for attention and heroism.

Now that Lillian has made her debut Joy must decide whether Lillian's shenanigans are warranted. Joy seeks comfort in her mirrored friend and begins to see just what her husband and conscious warned her about from the beginning. A hostile takeover is a foot as whispers of a million dollar check spark a loud chatter. Rumors of debt to some rather unsavory personalities, turn decent natures into scandalous rogues, desperation befalls party's trying to relinquish the debt. A plan is put into action to discredit Joy's right to Justin's estate.

Sam conjures a plan to get out of debt and build a nest egg of her own. While her husband Charles takes advantage of Joy's wavering consciousness. Both sisters look to uncover the missing link that has a hold on both Joy and Sam. Who will prevail? The truth unfolds as vengeful acts birth a sibling rivalry that tests the line between love and hate. The saga continues as Joy uncovers the myths of her family history and unveils the identity of her true Nemesis.